HAPPY MOSCOW

ANDREY PLATONOVICH PLATONOV (1899–1951) was the son of a railway worker. The eldest of ten children, he started work at the age of 15 as a mechanic and assistant engine driver. He began publishing poems and articles in 1918, at the same time as studying engineering. Throughout much of the 1920s he worked as a land reclamation expert. Between 1927 and 1932 he wrote his most politically controversial works, some of them first published in the Soviet Union only in the late 1980s. Other stories were published at the time, but subjected to vicious criticism. Stalin is reputed to have written "scum" in the margin of the story "For Future Use", and to have said to Fadeev (later to be Secretary of the Writers' Union), "Give him a good belting – for future use." During the 1930s Platonov made several confessions of error, but went on writing stories only marginally more acceptable to the authorities. His 15-year-old son was sent to the camps in 1938 and released three years later, only to die of the tuberculosis he had contracted there. During the Second World War Platonov worked as a war correspondent and published several volumes of stories, but came under attack again immediately after the war. He died in 1951, probably of tuberculosis caught from his son. To this day unpublished works continue to surface in Russian journals: *Happy Moscow*, which was never finished, was first published in Russia only in 1991, and a play, *Noah's Ark*, in 1993.

ROBERT CHANDLER's translations from the Russian include Vasily Grossman's *Life and Fate* and Igor Golomstock's *Totalitarian Art*. He is a co-translator of several volumes of Platonov, and the translator of the Everyman's Poetry editions of Sappho and Apollinaire.

ELIZABETH CHANDLER is a co-translator of two other volumes of Platonov, *The Return* and *The Portable Platonov*.

ANGELA LIVINGSTONE is a Research Professor at the University of Essex. She has published books on Pasternak and Lou Andreas Salome, is the translator of Marina Tsvetaeva's epic poem "The Ratcatcher" and her essays on poetry, and is a co-translator of *The Return* and *The Portable Platonov*.

NADYA BOUROVA's translations into Russian include stories by Edna O'Brien, Sean O'Casey and Virginia Woolf. She is a co-translator of *The Portable Platonov*.

ERIC NAIMAN teaches at the University of California, Berkeley. He is the author of *Sex in Public: The Incarnation of Early Soviet Ideology*.

Andrey Platonov

HAPPY MOSCOW

*Translated from the Russian by
Robert and Elizabeth Chandler,
with Angela Livingstone,
Nadya Bourova and Eric Naiman,
and with an Introduction by
Eric Naiman*

THE HARVILL PRESS
LONDON

First published in *Strana Filosofov III* in 1999

This edition first published in 2001 by
The Harvill Press
2 Aztec Row
Berners Road
London N1 0PW

www.harvill.com

1 3 5 7 9 8 6 4 2

English translation © Robert and Elizabeth Chandler, 2001
Introduction © Eric Naiman, 2001

A CIP catalogue record for this book
is available from the British Library

ISBN13 978 1 84555 342 4

Designed and typeset in Adobe Caslon at
Libanus Press, Marlborough, Wiltshire

Printed and bound in Great Britain by
CPI Antony Rowe, Chippenham and Eastbourne

CONTENTS

PREFACE

PLATONOV IS A MASTER, ONE OF THE GREATEST WRITERS
of the last century in any language. It is a privilege to have
the task of translating such remarkable work into English for the
first time.

The ideal translator of Platonov would be perfectly bilingual
and have an encyclopaedic knowledge of Soviet life. He would
be able to detect deeply buried allusions not only to the classics
of Russian and European literature, but also to speeches by
Stalin, to articles by such varied figures as Bertrand Russell and
Lunacharsky (the first Bolshevik Commissar for Enlightenment), to copies of Pravda from the thirties and to long-
forgotten minor works of Socialist Realism. He would be a
gifted and subtle punster. Most important of all, his ear for
English speech-patterns would be so perfect that he could
maintain the illusion of a speaking voice, or voices, even while
the narrator or the individual characters are using extraordinary
language or expressing extraordinary thoughts. Much has been
written about Platonov's creativity with language; not enough
has been written about the subtlety with which – even in
straight narrative – he reproduces the music of speech, its constantly shifting intonations and rhythms. If Platonov's command
of tone and idiom were less perfect, his linguistic experimenta-
tion would by now seem self-conscious and dated. In short,
Platonov is a poet, and almost every line of his finest work
poses problems for the translator. A perfect translation, like the
original, would sound not only extraordinary and shocking, but
also – in some indefinable way – right and natural.

I realized several years ago that I could translate Platonov only with an enormous amount of help from others. Translating can be lonely work; sharing the task with others has been a joy. And I feel Platonov would have enjoyed the thought of this volume being the product of collective labour. I am deeply grateful to all my co-translators: Nadya Bourova, with her near-perfect command of both English and Russian; my wife Elizabeth, with her sensitivity to matters of rhythm, idiom and tone; Angela Livingstone, with her profound understanding of the nature of translation and her refusal to settle for a plausible second-best; and Eric Naiman, with his sensitivity to word-play and his deep knowledge of Platonov's times.

I also wish to thank Anne Berkeley, Lucy Chandler, Olga Kouznetsova, Lars Lih, Mark Miller, Dorothy Schwarz and David Tugwell, all of whom have subjected every page of this translation to unusually attentive scrutiny. Flora and Igor Golomstock, Natalya Kornienko, Olga Makarova, Natalya Poltavtseva, and Valery Vyugin have helped with particular difficulties in the original. I have gained insights from Anne Coldefy-Faucard's French translation. Gabriel White, Eric Naiman's research assistant at the University of California, has made an invaluable contribution to the notes. I am also grateful to Clint Walker for allowing us to quote in our notes from his fine article about *Happy Moscow* (forthcoming in *Essays in Poetics*, Keele).

* * *

One further point: one of the most notoriously untranslatable Russian words is *toskà*. Vladimir Nabokov has written: "No single word in English renders all the shades of *toskà*. At its

viii

deepest and most painful, it is a sensation of great spiritual anguish, often without any specific cause. At less morbid levels it is a dull ache of the soul, a longing with nothing to long for, a sick pining, a vague restlessness, mental throes, yearning. In particular cases it may be the desire for somebody or something specific, nostalgia, lovesickness. At the lowest level it grades into ennui, boredom . . . "[1] Perhaps quixotically, we have decided in some instances to leave this word untranslated, to introduce Russian *toskà* to the pragmatic English. After all, if our language has room for *ennui*, why should it close the door to *toskà*?

* * *

Happy Moscow is unfinished. The original text was first published in *Novy Mir* No 9 (1991). The volume *Strana Filosofov III* (September 1999) includes a slightly different version of the text, prepared by Natalya Kornienko, which shows all of Platonov's changes and revisions to his manuscript. Except where indicated, this is the version we have followed.

ROBERT CHANDLER

INTRODUCTION

ANDREY PLATONOV WAS A GOOD LISTENER. EAGERLY, with both horror and tenderness, he eavesdropped on the changes in the Russian language that accompanied the incarnation of communist ideology. A voracious reader in the fields of philosophy, politics, science, technology and literature, Platonov hoped for the transformation of man and the universe, but he could not help mourning everything that would have to perish in that process: not only his fellow men but anything bearing the imprint of humanity. His work is about the exhilarating power of the language that was so radically transforming Russia in the first two decades of Soviet power, but also about the way in which this language distorted human lives and minds. In a variety of styles ranging from the hideous to the sentimental to the comic, Platonov laid bare the destruction wrought by ideology's attempts to remake both man and matter. Platonov makes us realize that no understanding of the Soviet "adventure" is possible unless one reflects upon the mutilating magic of words.

Platonov's mature works are often disconcerting to first-time readers. He was far more interested in philosophy and language than in plot. With the notable exception of *The Foundation Pit* (1930), his novels and longer stories are episodic and unconcerned with the development of character. His chief preoccupations are philosophical issues as reflected or, more often, distorted in the political rhetoric of his day. In a genre that might best be termed "the ideological picaresque" Platonov's heroes are philosophical "problems" such as the desire for moral purity, the relation of body to soul, the function of language, the meaning of materialism and – above all – the yearning for all-embracing community. Paradoxically, this craving for social unity is expressed in a loosely plotted form. Platonov's reluctance to depict the desire for social cohesion in a more structured form seems to arise from a belief that cohesion can be achieved only at the cost of excision and purification. Unwilling to exclude, Platonov keeps returning to things which have been left out, to the remnants and wastes produced by the demand for philosophical coherence.

I

Born on 1 September 1899, the eldest child of a railway worker in Voronezh, Platonov left school at the age of 15 to help support his large family. His work in a series of machine shops and factories was interrupted by the Revolution, which significantly expanded his horizon of expectations. In early 1918 he enrolled in the Railway Polytechnic, where he specialized in electrical engineering. He also began to publish prolifically in several local newspapers. His early articles cover a wide variety of topics and are typical of the time in their striking enthusiasm for the reconstruction of the entire cosmos. They betray a range of influences – from the movement for Proletarian Culture (the *Proletkul't*) sponsored by Aleksandr Bogdanov, to popular "decadent" Western thinkers such as Otto Weininger. Platonov also wrote poetry: short, sentimental verses that elegiacally celebrate maternity and nature, as well as wild proletarian fantasies that envision the fundamental remaking of nature in a world indistinguishable from a factory.

Though his father had a strong class sensibility, Platonov himself had attended a parish school and, like many authors in the *Proletkul't*, was not averse to using religious imagery and language. Unlike many other young proletarian writers, however, he appears to have read widely among the Russian spiritual philosophers active at the turn of the twentieth century. He was particularly impressed by Nikolay Fyodorov (1829–1903), a highly eccentric but influential thinker whose *Philosophy of the Common Task* proposed the physical resurrection of the dead as part of a massive spiritual and scientific undertaking that would combine the conquest of nature with the overcoming of the tragic modern split between mind and body. Essential to the success of this undertaking was the subjugation of sexual urges and the replacement of the sexual instinct by a pious imperative to *remember* (to recall and, quite literally, piece together) the dead. Less avowedly scientific, but equally utopian, the philosophical writings of Vladimir Solovyov (1853–1900) enshrined the related notions of "*sobornost* '" – social and spiritual collectivity – and "*vseedinstvo*" – all-encompassing unity. Like Fyodorov, Solovyov deplored sexual activity on the grounds that it led to people uniting on an animalistic and insufficiently communal basis and so impeded "all-penetrating" collectivity. Chastity was an essential step if mankind was to reach the highest, non-sexual level of love. Although neither Fyodorov nor Solovyov was a Marxist, their works had a strong appeal for the traditionally ascetic, self-sacrificing Russian intelligentsia, and their focus on the importance of community made their views susceptible to an improbable fusion with a Marxist-Leninist worldview.[2]

Another paradoxical influence for a young Communist writer was Russian Symbolism's preoccupation with the power of incantation. In the nineteenth century the limitations imposed on political expression had conferred upon literature in Russia a privileged status as a harbinger of, and vehicle for, social and economic change. In the first 15 years of the twentieth century, the Russian Symbolists took this notion further, finding in the popular, rural tradition of spells and incantations a model for more radical transformative expressions.[3] In the aesthetic manifestos of Andrey Bely and, later, Velimir Khlebnikov, language does not just reflect; it creates, or conjures, a world into being and is a primary sphere of voluntaristic endeavour.[4]

Although the Bolsheviks, as militant materialists, would never have acknowledged Bely or Khlebnikov as their avatars,[5] they too were enamoured of charismatic potential and prophetic, privileged voluntarism. They saw the Party's role as one of active intervention but, in the cataclysmic struggle engulfing Russia, words were as important as bullets; the newspapers and leaflets intended for barely literate workers and peasants constituted an essential second front.[6] Not surprisingly, the triumph of Bolshevism was easily envisioned as the victory of a new language. The official discourse, disseminated by authoritative Party and governmental organs, encompassed not only revolutionary acronyms, but also a new style of speaking (and thinking), a new stock of slogans, images and genres. Stalin's speeches accord tremendous importance to language itself: "Everyone is _talking_ about the successes of Soviet power in the area of the kolkhoz movement. [. . .] What does this all _say?_"[7] For Stalin, events were primarily discursive and metadiscursive, often to a dizzying degree: "Remember the latest events in our Party. Remember the latest _slogans_, which the Party has put forward lately in connection with the new class shifts in our country. I am _speaking_ about _slogans_, such as the _slogan_ of self-_criticism_, the _slogan_ of heightened struggle with bureaucracy and the purge of the Soviet apparatus, the _slogan_ of organization, etc."[8] In a country where everything is political, slogans become indistinguishable from events and are intended to have immediate consequences in the real world. (It is not for nothing that we speak of a Soviet *dictator*ship.) Essentially, one can see the entire premise of Socialist Realism – that writers, "the engineers of human souls", should show life in its "revolutionary unfolding" and thus speed the advent of the inevitable future – as a form of incantation.

In Platonov's early, journalistic period, he seems to have accepted uncritically the Marxist, spiritual and linguistic utopias available to him. His articles are imbued with the ideological fervour one would expect from a participant in the Civil War; at the same time they frequently incorporate a Solovyovian or Fyodorovan doctrine of self-negating brotherhood and chastity for which one would be hard-pressed to find a source in Marx. When more pragmatic policies were adopted by the Party soon after the Red Army's victory, Platonov seems to have voiced his disgust.[9] In late 1921 he was expelled from the Party, which he had joined just a year before. Platonov spent most of the first half of the decade engaged in engineering work; as a land reclamation specialist, he assisted in the planning and construction of a large number of dams and other irrigation projects. Yet he went on writing stories and articles, with a particular focus on what we might now call science fiction. In 1926 he moved to Moscow, where he continued to work as an engineer but also established himself as one of the most unusual figures on the Soviet literary scene: a genuinely proletarian writer whose peculiar use of ideological language generated profoundly ambivalent works. In his works of the late 1920s – most notably the novels *Chevengur* and *The Foundation Pit* – we find a writer who still subscribes, at some deep emotional level, to the utopian sentiments of his youth but who has become increasingly critical of the havoc created by the untempered pursuit of noble ideas. The heroes of *Chevengur* believe in an apocalyptic, quasi-religious utopia; as they strive to exterminate the local "bourgeoisie", they dream of universal brotherhood and of their own version of the Holy Grail: the corpse of Rosa Luxemburg. Their actions betray an inability to distinguish the literal and figurative dimensions of language; Platonov portrays these killers as horrifying, yet attractive, victims of utopian ideals and rhetoric. Don Quixote has returned as a collective of mass murderers. In both *Chevengur* and *The Foundation Pit* – which describes an attempt to create a gigantic home for the entire proletariat – the noble collectivist spirit is portrayed as ultimately suicidal. Sasha Dvanov, the hero of *Chevengur*, seeks a final incarnation of utopia in a watery grave, while Nastya, the little girl who symbolizes the hopes of the future, is buried in the ever-deepening foundation pit.

Platonov sent *Chevengur* to Maksim Gorky, who had been interested in his work ever since he read Platonov's first published collection of stories. Gorky was impressed by the power of Platonov's writing but criticized the "overly drawn-out" structure of the novel. More importantly, however, he pronounced the work unprintable in Soviet Russia:

> Publication will be prevented by your anarchic cast of mind, which is evidently inherent in the nature of your "spirit". Whether you wanted to or not, you have portrayed reality in a lyrical-satirical light, and that clearly is not acceptable to our censor. For all the tenderness of your attitude towards people, they are painted ironically by you, they appear before the reader not so much as revolutionaries, but as "cranks" and "half-wits".[10]

Neither *Chevengur* nor *The Foundation Pit* appeared in Russia until the time of *perestroika*. And when Platonov succeeded in publishing works in the leading literary journals, both he and the journals themselves inevitably attracted fierce criticism. For three years he was unable to publish a single story. A certain measure of redemption came only in 1934 when Platonov was included in a brigade of writers sent to Turkmenia. This trip led to the publication of one tale, though its major literary fruit, the novel *Dzhan*, remained unpublished for three decades.

2

Platonov began writing *Happy Moscow* during this period of enforced silence. His drafts and notebooks reveal that he began working on the novel in 1932 or 1933.[11] In early 1936 he signed a contract with a publishing house, but the novel never appeared. Platonov may have abandoned *Happy Moscow* because he realized that it was unpublishable, but we cannot be sure: his sense of what was or was not publishable had never been reliable. The abandonment of the novel coincided with the discovery of new outlets for stories and critical articles, and Platonov seems from this time to have directed his energy towards work in these less risky, smaller genres.

1933 began with Stalin's announcement that the first Five Year Plan had been fulfilled a year early. The following three or four years were a time of triumphalism. Socialism was declared to have achieved its "ultimate and irreversible victory" in Russia.[12] The Second Five-Year Plan brought a new focus on the joys of consumption. Earlier advertisements for Soviet products had invariably displayed images of the factories that produced them; now posters depicted happy families enjoying these products in the home.[13] The opening of facilities designed for the leisure of the socialist victors was heralded as a sign of the times; jazz halls and parks "of culture and rest" were part of a new lifestyle of pleasure suddenly available to, and even incumbent upon, all loyal Soviet subjects. The newspapers trumpeted the importance of each individual citizen to the success of the Soviet enterprise; in a 1935 speech Stalin attacked "indifference" to the fates of individuals and exhorted the graduates of the Red Army Academy to "learn to value people, to value cadres, to value each worker capable of contributing to our general good."[14] Stalin's speeches introduced the most quoted slogan of the period: "life has become better, life has become merrier".[15] The new focus on the enjoyment of life brought with it a demand for the cultivation of popular taste: newly urbanized peasants were instructed about what works of classical literature they should read, how they should groom themselves, how they should furnish their apartments (with tablecloths and lamp shades).[16] This campaign for "cultured life" (kul'turnost') was essentially a crash-course in the adoption of bourgeois practices, now repackaged as the tokens of socialist prosperity. "Happiness", a word previously coded as bourgeois and self-indulgent, became a marker of the fortunate condition of Soviet society as a whole. The word "prosperity", too, became a slogan of the day; Stalin used it to attack ascetic attitudes within the Party and the working class, declaring that "socialism can conquer only on the basis of the high productivity of labour, at a higher level than under capitalism, on the basis of an abundance of products and of all sorts of consumer goods, on the basis of a prosperous and cultured life for all members of society."[17]

The new high level of productivity was epitomized by the Stakhanovite movement: a campaign that encouraged increased economic output by loudly proclaiming the achievements of especially productive workers and rewarding them with new suits, record players, radios and – above all – trips to Moscow. Moscow became the consummate symbol of the Stalinist paradise; the city was torn apart by new building projects, the most prominent of which may have been the construction of the Moscow Metropolitan. The city was portrayed in books and movies as a fairy-tale capital; a place where "cultured" dreams came true. All this, of course, was a myth; living standards remained low, the Stakhanovite movement generated rising production norms that most workers could not possibly meet, and the Soviet Union grew ever more repressive.[18] Yet this depiction of prosperity was entirely in keeping with the doctrine of Socialist Realism, enshrined by the First Congress of the Union of Writers in 1934. Writers were supposed to reflect in present-day surroundings the rapidly approaching world of the future, and in the fulfilment of this task they were joined by film-makers and, above all, journalists. Even the cartographers took part; the German immigrant Wolfgang Leonhard later recalled that when he arrived in Moscow in the mid-1930s, he had to orient himself by using the only two maps he could find: one published in 1925 and the other, more recent, showing how the city would look in the mid-1940s.[19]

Concomitant with the enshrining of pleasure as a token of ascendant communism was a reaccentuation of the fertile female form and the reproductive body. Sexuality had been a topic of great ideological concern in the 1920s, where it was often seen as a threat to the communist enterprise. Now sexual reproduction – the demographic proof of collective joy – was the order of the day. As Stalin put it in characteristically cheery fashion:

Now everyone here is saying that the material condition of workers has significantly improved, that life has become better, happier. This, of course, is true. But this is causing the population to reproduce much faster than in olden times. Mortality has fallen, the birth rate is up, and the demographic gain is thus incomparably greater, This, of course, is good, and we applaud it. (*Merry animation in the hall.*)

Platonov was deeply disturbed by this focus on merriment, pleasure and prosperity. In "Among Animals and Plants",[20] a savage, moving story written at this time, he inverts the stereotypical plot of More's *Utopia*, where the ideal (and, lest we forget, satirically portrayed) society is a remote island hidden from the "normal" world. In Platonov's story, the hero is a worker on an isolated railway line in the North who "understands" (through the radio, newspapers and books) that a paradise has been built and exists *all around him* but is himself unable to see or sense it. He obtains access to this world only when he stages an accident, cripples himself in saving his fellow workers from injury and is rewarded with a trip to Moscow. (His wife, apparently thinking of the likes of Moscow Chestnova, is afraid he will meet pretty parachutists there!) Self-mutilation is seen as the admission ticket to the new utopia.

The slogans of the mid-1930s seem to have reawakened the ascetic tendencies that were so strong in the young Platonov; *Happy Moscow* and other writings portray the new Soviet preoccupation with pleasure as virtually obscene. In an article sent to Gorky but unpublished until just a few years ago, Platonov explained one aspect of his dissatisfaction:

One must not thrust oneself forward and get drunk on life: our time is better and more serious than blissful pleasure. Every one who gets drunk will be caught and will perish without fail – like a little mouse, who crawls into a mousetrap, in order to "get drunk" on the lard used as bait. There is a lot of lard around us, but every piece is bait.[21]

Platonov saw the essence of "socialist tragedy" (the title of his article) in contemporary man's lack of readiness to cope with the power of technology. Technology was fast allowing man to regulate all-important elemental processes, but man was still inadequate to these tasks and so susceptible to all sorts of physical and ideological temptations. Ideology, Platonov explained in the same article, "is located not on an external height, not in the 'superstructure', but in the very heart of man and in the centre of his social being".

In essence, *Happy Moscow* is about the gulf between, on the one hand, the technology and even the language of "triumphant" socialism, and, on the other hand, human souls, hearts and minds. Socialism is hollow if it is only for the best and the brightest and does not concern itself with those in danger of being left behind. The desire for happiness is natural, but happiness ought not to be exclusive, nor should it be founded on either egotism or abstractions. Happiness should come from a (still elusive) compatibility of ideology and the heart; abstract schemes for social transformation will bring benefit only if informed by intimate love for other human beings and the physical world. *Happy Moscow* castigates the premature, triumphant celebration of individual and pseudo-collective pleasure; at the same time, "thinking two thoughts at once", the novel reveals the painful price paid by individual ascetics who love the whole of humanity so much that they are ashamed of intimacy with another person and even of the material necessity of having (or being) a self.

3

The hero of Platonov's novel is not so much an individual woman as the idea and the language of Collectivity. Moscow herself (as a synecdoche for the metropolitan showcase and thus for the Soviet ideal as a whole) is a kind of Every Citizen; repeatedly she is introduced to the reader obliquely – a woman is described in a particular situation and then – presto! – that woman turns out to be Moscow Chestnova. Moving from one occupation to the next, Moscow represents the antithesis of bourgeois (and novelistic!) individualism; her identity is unfixed, she repeatedly reincarnates.

Moscow desires to participate in every aspect of the new world taking shape around her. She takes seriously (and absurdly!) the Dostoevskian dictate that "All are responsible for all" and longs to ensure that absolutely everything functions well – from the heating of water in the pipes of dance-hall showers, to the driving of piles into the Moscow River, to the conception of "new people". (In Dostoevsky's formulation all people are responsible for one another; Moscow, as a devoted materialist, is also responsible for the functioning of all technology and all *things*.) As a woman, she selflessly gives herself to one man after another, becoming a sexual hypostasis of the communal ideal, the home where there will always be room for someone else to fit.[22] Indeed, as an object of desire, she embodies the yearning encouraged by Stalinist ideology – Moscow as the ideal centre which the entire nation strives to penetrate. (Her lovers seem to be acting in accordance with the famous Chekhovian refrain "*V Moskvu, v moskvu*" – (in)to Moscow, (in)to Moscow.) Moscow's sexual activity parodies the Solovyovian ideal of collectivity, or, more accurately, it shows how debased that notion has become in Stalin's Russia. Not unexpectedly, *Happy Moscow* depicts sexual union as unsatisfying; true to Solovyov's paradigm, those who engage in it feel less, rather than more unified with the surrounding community.[23] (After having sexual relations with Moscow, Sartorius feels only "indifference to the interests of life".) In the terminology of Otto Weininger, whom Platonov read avidly both in his youth and later,[24] Moscow is an embodiment of both "types" of women – the Mother and the Prostitute. Her relationship to the world is not only sexual but umbilical: "had it been possible to connect the whole world to it, her heart could have regulated the course of events". Paradoxically, Moscow's sexual promiscuity is a kind of ideological asceticism. She does not allow herself to find happiness with a single man, because she feels compelled to devote herself to everyone around her. What good is her life to her, she asks, "without the whole of the USSR?"

At the novel's conclusion, Sartorius follows Moscow in attempting to transcend the limits of individuality; he changes his identity, finds a new job, gives himself a crash-course in Stalinist "culturedness" and moves in with a new wife and family. Finally he buys someone else's passport, disappears from Platonov's text, and the novel refers to him henceforth only as "Grunyakhin"; language and, above all, the language of official documents, is a serious matter.[25]

Platonov understands that the Soviet corruption of the communist ideal has occurred in large measure through the degradation of language. The word *obshchiy* (meaning "general," "shared," "mutual" or "common") is accorded exceptional prominence in this novel about community. Occasionally the word passes by almost imperceptibly, in common idioms, or as part of compound words which reveal themselves to be ideological puns only when examined more closely. Thus, for example, the young Moscow writes her essay for school *za obshchim stolom* ("at the shared table"), she begins to study at the aviation school and moves into an *obshchezhitie* ("hostel", literally, a place of "living in common"): a symbolic transition from the narrow confines of "chance" marriage to the joys of collective life. Bozhko's correspondents are too poor to travel, but "*so-obshcha[yutsya] drug s drugom myslyu*" ("communicate with one another through thought"). Bozhko consoles his correspondents with the news that "the common property (*obshchee dobro*) of the working people grows day by day". Moscow's selflessness and promiscuity is subtly figured in "*v obshchem ona byla khorosha i nich'ya*" ("*all in all*, she was good-looking, and she belonged to nobody"). Even where the word *obshchiy* is used idiomatically, its frequent repetition eventually makes of it a mere ideological mantra, devalued through overuse. At other points *obshchiy* surfaces in odd, non-idiomatic contexts that immediately attract attention. Moscow is summoned into the strangely sounding "*obshchiy letniy sumrak*" (literally, "shared summer dusk"). The woman whom both Bozhko and Sartorius know (Lisa's mother) is strangely referred to as their "*obshchaya starukha*" (literally "shared little old woman"). What all these characters most truly share is a hideous common tongue that affects every moment of their lives. They do not need Esperanto, for they are already fluent in the Soviet Union's own artificial tongue.

The theme of filth and excrement appears elsewhere in

Platonov's work but is particularly prominent in *Happy Moscow*, where it operates on two different levels: the sentimental and the satiric. Dirt and excrement are regarded affectionately as a symbolic counterpart of the proletariat in Marx's dynamic of class relations;[26] a truly humanistic communism is obliged to care for everything – even the excrement that is the material manifestation of the "insulted and injured". In the context of the Russian philosophical tradition, filth serves as the counterpart of Nikolay Fyodorov's ancestral "dust" which must be lovingly located and preserved until the moment of scientific resurrection. Sartorius smells Moscow's shoes and even touches them with his tongue; if he had the opportunity, he would look "at the waste products of her body with the greatest of interest, since they too had not long ago formed part of a splendid person". He thinks of Moscow "with such tenderness that if Moscow had squatted down to pee, Sartorius would have begun to cry". Rarely has the language of sentimentalism been put to such use! Moscow herself is described as a kind of organic machine that transforms filth into beauty. As she washes, she marvels "at the chemistry of nature that could turn ordinary, scant food (and what filth had she not eaten in her life!) into the rosy purity and blossoming expanses of her body". While listening to the sounds of Komyagin copulating, Moscow presses her chest against a cold sewer pipe; in a gesture of physical contact parallel to – but spiritually *higher* than – Komyagin's, she is embracing all that "the upper floor" of society discards. Later, Sartorius displays a spiritual kinship with Moscow by leaning his head against this same sewer pipe and hearing in it "the intermittent sound of filth flowing down from the upper floors". Sambikin demonstrates a similar affection for waste when he has Moscow's leg sent to his house; indeed, his entire experimental project is founded on the notion that the origins of life must be sought in filth. Sambikin considers the possibility of marrying a female corpse, while Sartorius is aroused by dreams of Moscow "wretched, or already dead, lying in poverty on the eve of her burial"; these interchangeable male protagonists are both attracted by death and decay.[27]

Many of Platonov's mature works are structured around a fundamental pun that expresses the central philosophical preoccupation of the author. Such puns are not made the explicit object of authorial attention but provide a frame for the ideological "action" in a particular work. The central pun in *Happy Moscow* is the transformation of Solovyov's ideal of *sobornost'* (collectivity) into *ubornost'* (from the word "*ubornaya*", meaning "latrine", from the verb *ubirat'/ubrat'*: "to take away, to clean up"). This collectivity of the toilet is a paradoxical notion, since Platonov is serious about the importance of the downtrodden whom society is in the process of evacuating. Bozhko's insistence on collecting every crumb dropped by his beloved land "in order that the country should survive in its entirety", represents a relatively non-parodic vision of collectivity, as does his epistolary activity, described – in a phrase redolent of the Symbolist worldview – as "world-wide *correspondence*". But the description of Bozhko's quarters shows us that this devotion to wretchedness is taken to an extreme: "the room's furnishings [*ubranstvo*, from the verb *ubrat'*, to clean up] were poor and austere – not because of poverty but because of dreaminess. There was an iron bed like in an epidemic ward, with a greasy blanket impregnated through and through with humanity; a bare table fit for great concentration; a mass-produced chair that had been salvaged from somewhere or other; home-made shelves against the wall, with the best books of socialism and of the nineteenth century, and three portraits above the table – Lenin, Stalin and Doctor Zamenhof." In his devotion to these portraits as well as to the bed and blanket stained with the sickness and suffering of humanity, Bozhko insists upon the essential importance of a link between the wretched and the lofty; his ideals, however, are subverted by the literalness with which he embodies them.

Of course, Platonov's use of toilet imagery, and the replacement of *sobornost'* by *ubornost'*, serves, too, as a satirical commentary on the kind of collectivity achieved in Stalinist society, where privilege and pleasure enjoy ideological pride of place. The Stakhanovites are depicted as new aristocrats; for them to dress in poor or dirty clothing would be a rebuke to the land that adorns its "best people" with "the choicest goods" ("*otbornym dobrom*") and places them among "rich furnishings" ("*bogatoe ubranstvo*"). The Soviet Union of the 1930s has been purified, tidied up; there is no longer a place in it for those who do not fit the bright, shining image of the new men and women being produced by Socialist Realism. Moscow explains to Sambikin that she attached herself to Komyagin because she "had begun to feel ashamed of living among her former friends, in their shared, orderly city (*v obshchem ubrannom gorode*), now that she was lame, thin and mentally not right in the head. So she had decided to hide away in the room of someone she knew, someone poor, to wait until time had passed and she could be merry again." The logic of the process of ideological cleansing to which Moscow, the city, and the USSR are being subjected is that it will eventually lead not only to the elimination of the physically and ideologically deficient but to the destruction of life itself. Sambikin does not entirely rid his young patient's body of infection because he understands that "the complete destruction of the streptococci would entail cutting to pieces not only the whole of the patient's head but also his entire body right down to his toenails." The same insight colours the novel's treatment of the philosophically important distinction between body and soul. Solovyov had founded his notion of collective harmony on a "spiritualization of matter",[28] an overcoming of the body-soul antithesis that would lift matter out of its currently degraded state. Platonov seems suspicious of this "solution", because in essence it destroys matter under the pretence of redeeming it. Sambikin asserts that the soul resides in the intestines, in the empty space between the food that has not yet been assimilated and "the remnants of excrement".[29] By situating the soul so close to filth, Platonov ensures that the body is not left behind, that ideological language never loses contact with the lowest form of matter. With a note of melancholy realism, Bozhko implores Sartorius: "It's true: we must remake the whole world and make everything splendid. Think of all the filth that has seeped into humanity during the thousands of years we've been like animals! Something's got to be done with it all. Even our body's not the way it should be – it's full of dirt."

The body cannot be cleaned up without destroying it, and wastes cannot simply be taken away. Rather, filth is the proletariat of the cosmos and must be collected and cherished. For Platonov, ideological purity entails simultaneously striving for the heavens and immersing oneself in dirt.

Even before she loses her leg, Moscow is repelled by the new discourse of personal satisfaction, individual cultural development and pleasure:

> [She saw] joy or contentment almost everywhere yet [felt] sadder and sadder herself. Everyone was occupied solely by mutual egotism with their friends, by their

favourite ideas, by the warmth of their new rooms and the comfortable feeling of their own satisfaction. Moscow did not know what to attach herself to, whom to go and see, in order to live happily and normally. There was no joy for her in houses, she found no peace in the warmth of stoves or the light of table-lamps.

"The whole of life" (*vseobshchaya zhizn'*) passes by her, "so petty and rubbishy" that she sees how isolated people are and how "the space between them [is] occupied by bewilderment". Moscow visits an all-night restaurant and dance hall, which represents the height of the pursuit of individual pleasure. An orchestra plays mindless European music, so centrifugal that "you felt like curling your body up for warmth and lying down for a long time in a narrow, secluded coffin". This description of hell is audaciously marked by the key word of the decade, "merriment":

> The later time got and the more the merriment thickened, the quicker the spherical hall of the restaurant began to revolve; forgetting where the door was, many of the guests span round in terror on the spot, somewhere in the middle of the hall, supposing they were dancing.

This is a highly symbolic moment: we should read it as Platonov's comment on the ideological mood of his age. *Revolution* has given way to a terrified, self-indulgent spinning – repetition without progress – that will ultimately lead to its participants' destruction. At the evening's end, the hall has been "devastated by long merriment as if by some cataclysm".

The discourse of merriment appears in other contexts. For example, Sartorius looks out of the window and sees "whole crowds of people . . . travelling by in trams, on their way home from theatres and from visiting their friends". These passers-by "felt merry in one another's company and could count on their lives getting better". Writers were supposed to depict life in a manner consistent with Party pronouncements, but this sentence is such a literal "reflection" of Stalin's oft-quoted slogan that it appears ludicrous, even parodic – not only of Stalin but also of the manner in which writers were supposed to provide narrative scripts for the Party line. Moreover, this merry new life has begun to look a lot like bourgeois individualism. Sartorius is well paid for his inventions; "with this money he dressed Lisa in luxury [and] for some time he lived lightheartedly, even merrily, devoting himself to love, theatre-going, and pleasures of the moment". Most disturbing of all, perhaps, is the suggestion that the new merriment is a form of living death. Sambikin sits up late with "some dead matter" and tries "to extract the little-known, merry substance which had been stored up inside it, ready for a long life that had failed to happen". Is the new merry substance little more than dead matter? The collectivity that results is one which seems to neglect humanity, to transform communists into mere "*zhil'tsy*" – tenants or, etymologically, people who are merely living – rather than fully *human* beings. When Sartorius stands in the hallway pressing his head to the sewer pipe, nobody notices him: "Now and again tenants would go down the corridor to the communal toilet (*obshchaya ubornaya*), but they paid no particular attention to the unknown human being in the darkness . . ."

Human beings are ignored, while collectivity has gone to the toilet.

The language of *Happy Moscow* merits an entire essay of its own; here a few additional comments must suffice. Much of Platonov's brilliance as a writer derives from his audacious mixing of stylistic levels; the effect is often hilarious, even when the subject matter is brutal or grotesque. *Happy Moscow* brims with stylistically absurd phrases, such as "the year when wars all ended and the transportation system began to function again", where the first part of the phrase is reminiscent of folk tale, and the second part belongs to the lexicon of bureaucrats or journalists. A similar dynamic is at work in the remark: "it was music she lived for, not the digestion of food", where a term for a biological process sits restlessly in what we expect to be a pithy maxim. Komyagin expresses his desire to learn about death in bureaucratic language ("where and according to what procedures a man is finally excluded from the register of citizens") interlarded with more casual and subjective formulations. Komyagin's denunciation of his own character reads like a deranged thesaurus: "I'm vanishing. I'm an old song. My itinerary's nearing its end. Soon I shall collapse into the hollow of personal death." The purpose of this stylistic tactic is to show the way in which incompatible discourses warp the consciousness of people desperate for the rewards of ideological enlightenment. Platonov's characters are unable to use different registers of speech for different aspects of their lives; part of the horror of totalitarianism is its demand that ideology inform all areas of human existence, that all areas of life be talked about in the same way. There is no escape from the master tongue. A touching but comical moment occurs when Sartorius hears one of Komyagin's neighbours whisper the prayer: "Remember me, Lord, in thy kingdom, as I remember thee. And grant me something factual – I beg you!" (*day mne chto-nibud' fakticheskoe*). This poor tenant is seeking relief from his squalid life and asks, as a Russian Symbolist poet might have done, for something genuine, something more real than the base world into which the spirit has fallen. Yet even though this man begins his prayer with traditional liturgical language, he can ask for the "real" only in the language of Stalin's speeches, with their obsessive reference to "facts".

Occasionally, Platonov will employ a pun for its own, purely comic sake, but often a pun contains an important philosophical comment or captures a fundamental ideological opposition. For example, we learn that Sartorius "intended to use events and circumstances to destroy the resistance of his personality, so that the unknown feelings of other people could enter him one by one". Here the fulcrum of the sentence is the opposition of the word for individual personality (*lichnost'*) to the word for event (*sobytie*) which literally means co-being: exactly the ideal Sartorius desires to attain. Similarly, at first Sambikin loves Moscow, but then he begins "to puzzle over her, as if she were some problem" (*dumal nad ney, kak nad problemoy*). Given the sexualized nature of virtually all Moscow's relations with men, the reader does not know whether to take this "over her" in a literal or figurative sense; more important, however, is the fact that Moscow is indeed a "problem". In the terminology of the Russian formalists, Platonov is "baring his device": Moscow is as much a philosophical and ideological conundrum as she is a woman.

Platonov's sentences often appear to contain redundant elements, but this redundancy has a purpose: the seemingly unnecessary words puffing up a sentence often add philosophical or ideological complexity. Thus, chapter two opens with the words: "In the centre of the capital, on the seventh floor, lived a 30-year-old man, Viktor Vasilievich Bozhko" ("*zhil tridtsatiletniy chelovek Viktor Vasil'evich Bozhko*"). Platonov might easily and more naturally have omitted the word "man", yet its introduction is important to the novel's central theme of humanity and its stubborn resistance to ideological schemes: Bozhko, perhaps more than any of the characters, is determined to be *a human being*, a term that implies dignity, virtue and compassion rather than automatic membership in a species.[30]

One of the most fascinating techniques employed by Platonov is his narrativization of Bolshevik rhetoric. Platonov read the ideological pronouncements of his day closely and appears to have paid special attention to Stalin's speeches. So, of course, did many other writers; what is unique about Platonov's writing is his way of recontextualizing Stalin's rhetoric in ludicrous and parodic ways. Let us take the scene where Moscow tries to light a cigarette in the midst of her leap with a parachute:

> Moscow opened the door of the aeroplane and took her step into emptiness; a fierce vortex struck at her from below . . . Moscow felt she was an empty tube, with the wind blowing right through her, and she kept her mouth constantly open so she would manage to breathe out this savage wind that was piercing right into her . . . She took out a cigarette and some matches, wanting to light up and have a smoke, but the match went out; Moscow then curled up to make a quiet, comfortable space by her bosom and immediately exploded all the matches in the box; carried by the pull of the vortex, flames seized the combustible lacquer impregnating the silk straps

which linked the weight of the human being to the canopy of the parachute; these straps burnt away in less than a moment, immediately turning white-hot and scattering into ash. Moscow did not see what happened to the canopy because the wind was now burning the skin on her face, as a result of the brutal, ever-increasing speed of her fall downwards.

She flew, her cheeks red and burning . . . She pulled the ring of the reserve parachute, caught sight of the ground of the aerodrome, with its signal lights, and let out a cry of sudden torment – the opening parachute had jerked her body upwards with such force that a pain like raging toothache had suddenly shot through all her bones. Two minutes later she was sitting on the grass, covered by the parachute, and she began to crawl out from under it, wiping away the tears that had been forced from her by the wind.

Moscow crawls out from under the parachute "a national celebrity"; her emergence is treated as a kind of birth. (The word used by Platonov for "canopy" is also part of the term for the amniotic sac.) Even though her jump has been a spectacular failure, Moscow is accorded the glory and privileges of a young Stakhanovite. This entire episode perplexed the well-known contemporary writer Yury Nagibin: "Can you imagine a smoking parachutist? Moreover, Moscow does not smoke; nowhere else in the novel, neither before nor after the jump, does she touch a cigarette. And here she lights up in mid-air, using an entire box at once, and ignites the chute. This is not the act of Moscow, but the act of an author who needs it for his own purposes and not for the purposes of a character."[31] The motivation for this episode becomes clear when we examine a 1935 speech by Stalin:

> First of all, one's eyes are struck by the fact that the Stakhanovite movement began somehow on its own, in an almost *elemental* fashion, *from below*, without any pressure from our factories' administrations. [. . .] Therefore, the Stakhanovite movement *was born* and developed as a movement from *below*. Precisely because it was born of its own volition, precisely because it comes *from below*, it seems to be the most vital and unconquerable meaning of contemporaneity. It follows that we should also dwell on another characteristic trait of the Stakhanovite movement. This characteristic trait is that the Stakhanovite movement has spread *across the whole face* of our Union – not gradually but with some sort of unseen speed, like a *hurricane*. [. . .] And suddenly – the flame of the Stakhanovite movement has taken possession of the whole country. What is going on? Whence the rapidity of the spreading of the Stakhanovite movement? [. . .] You have seen Stakhanov and Busygin [another Stakhanovite]. These are simple, modest people. It even seems to me that they are somewhat embarrassed by the wide scope of the movement, which has unfurled beyond their expectations. And if, despite this, *the matches thrown by Stakhanov and Busygin have been sufficient to allow this movement to burst forth in flame*, that means that the Stakhanovite movement is something that has been ripening to full maturity.[32]

Platonov has transposed Stalin's rhetoric into an absurd narrative, and Moscow's enactment of Stalin's metaphors – a strong wind "from below" blowing "across Moscow's face", the comparison of the Stakhanovite movement to both a birth and the sudden ignition of a flame from matches – leads to nearly disastrous consequences. Platonov's point in staging this narrative exercise is to emphasize the strange relationship between language and reality in Socialist Realism and Stalin's Russia, where language did not just reflect reality but dictated it. What Platonov does in *Happy Moscow* is to take ideological dictation, endowing ideological figures with fantastic novelistic flesh. When Moscow listens to "great and humane" music, she hears it "as though it were both the Leader's speech and her own words". Platonov's prose is a strange amalgam of the leader's discourse and *his* own words; it is often comic, frequently grotesque, at once amazingly creative and tragically crippled.

In a despairing letter to his wife written in the mid-1930s, Platonov describes himself as "inharmonious and misshapen", a sentiment he conveys in a poster glimpsed by Moscow on the walls of Komyagin's housing co-operative: "a man shaped like the letter Я, one of his legs cut short by a road accident". This is an extremely significant image. In his notebooks for 1931, Platonov observed: "The new world really exists, in as much as there is a generation of people sincerely thinking and acting on the plane of orthodoxy, on the plane of an animated 'poster', – but it is local, [exists] alongside other countries [. . .] and cannot be world-wide or universally historic."[33] Moscow Chestnova begins as an animated cardboard reproduction of the new world, but she soon becomes a poster child for a quite different sort of existence. The same might be said for *Happy Moscow* itself, which opens with a Promethean image of October 1917 and eventually exposes Prometheus as Komyagin. A similar dynamic applies to the relation between Platonov's heroes and the land in which they live. The well-intentioned, foolish but essentially happy Foma Pukhov of Platonov's earlier novella, "*Sokrovenniy chelovek*" ("The Innermost Man" or "The Cherished Man") has given way to this "*sokrashchenniy chelovek*", an "abridged man" in a world with far less hope. Finally, since, standing alone, the letter Я means "I" in Russian, we can see this image of a physically abridged "man shaped like the letter Я" as a self-reflexive comment by the author, a writer both abridged and empowered by his time.[34] The distortion of men and of language was central to everything of value that Andrey Platonov wrote. In both form and content, his work captures the strange combination of enthusiasm and catastrophe that characterized Russia in the twentieth century.

ERIC NAIMAN

HAPPY MOSCOW

I

A DARK MAN WITH A BURNING TORCH WAS RUNNING
down the street on a bleak night in late autumn. The little girl
saw him through a window of her home as she woke from a
bleak dream. Then she heard a powerful shot from a rifle and
a poor, sad cry – the man running with the torch had probably been killed. Soon afterwards came the sound of distant,
repeated shots and of uproar from the nearby prison. The little
girl went back to sleep and everything she saw during the following days got forgotten: she was too small, and the memory
and mind of early childhood became overgrown for ever in her
body by subsequent life. But until her last years the nameless
running man would appear unexpectedly and sadly inside her –
in the pale light of memory – and perish once again in the dark
of the past, in the heart of a grown-up child. Amid hunger or
sleep, at a moment of love or some youthful joy – suddenly the
sad cry of the dead man was there again in the distance, deep in
her body, and the young woman would immediately change her
life: if she was dancing, she would stop dancing; if she was working, she would work more surely, with more concentration; if
she was alone, she would cover her face with her hands. On that
rainy night in late autumn the October Revolution had begun –
in the city where Moscow Ivanovna Chestnova was then living.

Her father died from typhoid and the hungry, orphaned
girl went out of the house and never went back there again.
Remembering neither people nor space, her soul gone to sleep,
for several years she walked and ate up and down her country,
as if her motherland were a void, until she found herself in a

children's home and at school. She was sitting at a desk by a window, in the city of Moscow. The trees on the boulevard had stopped growing; leaves were falling from them without any wind, covering up the now silent earth for its long sleep to come. It was the end of September, and the year when wars all ended and the transportation system began to function again.

Moscow Chestnova had been in the children's home for two years. It was here that she had been given a name, a surname and even a patronymic, since she had only the vaguest memory of her own name and early childhood. She thought her father had called her Olya, but she had not been sure of this and had kept silent, as though she were nameless, like that man in the night who had died. So she had been given a first name in honour of Moscow, a patronymic in memory of all the Ivans who had died in battle as ordinary Red Army soldiers, and a surname in recognition of the honesty[1] of her heart – which had not had time to become dishonest, in spite of long unhappiness.

The clear and ascending life of Moscow Chestnova had begun as she sat by the window on that autumn day in her second year at school, watching the death of the leaves on the boulevard and reading with interest a sign on the house opposite: A. V. KOLTSOV[2] WORKERS' AND PEASANTS' LIBRARY AND READING ROOM. Before the last lesson the children had each been given white bread for the first time in their lives, along with a meat patty and some potato, and told that the patties were made from cows. At the same time they were told to write a composition for the next day about a cow – if they had ever seen one – and about their future life. In the evening Moscow Chestnova, now full of white bread and dense patty, was writing

4

her composition at the shared table; her friends had all gone to sleep and the small electric lamp gave only a faint light.

Story by a Girl with no Father or Mother about her Future Life: We are being taught to have minds, but minds are in heads, there is nothing on the outside. We must labour to live truthfully, I want to live the future life, I want there to be biscuits and jam and sweets and always to be able to walk by the trees in the fields. Otherwise I won't live, I won't feel like it. I want to live normally with happiness. There's nothing to say in addition.

Later Moscow ran away. She was brought back after a year and was held up to shame at a meeting of the whole school: how could she, a daughter of the Revolution, behave in such an unethical and undisciplined manner?

"I'm not a daughter, I'm an orphan!" Moscow answered – and once again began studying diligently, as though she had not been away anywhere at all.

What she liked most in nature were the wind and the sun. She liked to lie in the grass, to listen to what the wind, like someone unseen and full of yearning, was saying in the thick of the bushes, and to see the summer clouds float by high above all the unknown countries and peoples. Observing clouds and space made Moscow's heart beat more rapidly in her chest, as if her body had been carried up to a great height and left there on its own. Then she would wander through fields, over simple, poor land, looking carefully and keenly all round her, still getting used to being alive in the world, and feeling glad that everything in it was right for her – for her body, her heart, and her freedom.

After completing her nine years of school, Moscow, like every young person, began unconsciously looking for the path into her future, towards happy closeness with other people; her hands longed for activity, her feelings sought dignity and heroism, and in her mind some still-mysterious but exalted fate was already triumphing. The 17-year-old Moscow could not go in anywhere on her own; she was waiting for an invitation, as if she valued the gift of youth and the strength that had grown up in her. And so, for some time, she became lonely and strange. Then a chance man got to know Moscow and won her over with his feelings and his courtesy, and she married him, immediately and for ever spoiling her body and her youth. Her large hands, fit for bold activity, were taken up with embraces; her heart, which had looked for heroism, began to love just one sly man who kept a tight hold on her, as if she were some inalienable asset. But one morning Moscow felt so achingly ashamed of her life, not quite knowing exactly why, that she kissed her sleeping husband on the forehead by way of farewell and left their room, not even taking a change of clothes. Until evening she wandered along the boulevards and along the bank of the Moscow River, sensing only the drizzle and wind of September and not think- ing anything, because she was empty and tired.

She wanted, as in her wandering childhood, to find some kind of box or empty food-stall to sleep in, but she found she had long grown too big and that there was nowhere she could squeeze into without being seen. She sat down on a bench in the darkness of the late-night boulevard and dozed off, listening to the mutterings of the thieves and homeless toughs who were wandering about nearby.

At midnight an insignificant-looking man sat down on the same bench, with the secret and ashamed hope that this woman might suddenly fall in love with him, since he himself was too meek to search for love with any persistence. He was not really looking for beauty of face or charm of figure – he was ready to agree to anything and to make any sacrifice if only someone would respond to him with true feeling.

"What do you want?" asked Moscow, who had woken up.

"Nothing," the man answered. "Nothing at all."

"I want to sleep, and I've nowhere to go," said Moscow.

The man immediately told her that he had a room. So she would not mistrust his intentions, however, he suggested she take a room in a hotel and sleep there in a clean bed, curled up in a blanket. Moscow agreed and they set off. On the way Moscow instructed her companion to get her enrolled in some place of study, with a hostel and canteen.

"What do you love most of all?" he asked.

"I love the wind in the air and a few other things," said the exhausted Moscow.

"Then it's got to be the school of aeronautics – that and nothing else!" concluded Moscow's companion. "I'll do my best."

He found a room for her in the Minin House, paid for three nights in advance, gave Moscow 30 roubles for food and set off home, carrying away within him his own consolation.

Five days later, thanks to his efforts, Moscow entered the school of aeronautics and moved to the hostel.

2

IN THE CENTRE OF THE CAPITAL, ON THE SEVENTH floor, lived a 30-year-old man, Viktor Vasilievich Bozhko.[3] He lived in a small room lit by a single window; the din of the new world reached his high-up abode like a symphonic composition – the falsehood of mean and mistaken sounds was extinguished before it could rise any higher than the fourth floor. The room's furnishings were poor and austere – not because of poverty but because of dreaminess. There was an iron bed like in an epidemic ward, with a greasy blanket impregnated through and through with humanity; a bare table fit for great concentration; a mass-produced chair that had been salvaged from somewhere or other; home-made shelves against the wall, with the best books of socialism and of the nineteenth century, and three portraits above the table – Lenin, Stalin and Doctor Zamenhof, the inventor of the international language of Esperanto.[4] Below these portraits, in four rows, hung small photographs of nameless people; there were not only white faces, but also Negroes, Chinese and inhabitants of every country.

Until late into the evening the room stayed empty; tired, sad sounds would gradually die away in it, languishing substance would let out little creaks and cracks; a quadrilateral of sunlight, shaped by the window, would slowly creep across the floor and fade into night as it reached the wall. Everything comes to an end, only objects are left to pine in the dark.

Then the man who lived there would arrive, and ignite the technological light of electricity. As usual, he would be happy and calm, because his life was not passing by in vain; his body was tired from the day, his eyes had lost their colour, but his heart was beating rhythmically and his thoughts were as clear and sparkling as they had been that morning. Bozhko, a geometrician and town planner, had that day completed a meticulous plan for a new residential street, allocating space for greenery, children's playgrounds and a district stadium. Anticipating a future that was close at hand, he felt the heartbeat of happiness as he worked, though he looked on himself with indifference, since he was a man who had been born under capitalism.

Bozhko took out a file of the personal letters he received almost every day at his office and, sitting at the empty table, began to focus his mind on them. He received letters from Melbourne, Cape Town, Hong-Kong and Shanghai, from small islands hiding in the watery waste of the Pacific, from Egypt, from Megarida – a hamlet at the foot of Mount Olympus in Greece – and from countless other places in Europe. Clerks and factory workers, far-off men trodden into the ground by eternal exploitation, had learned Esperanto and so conquered the silence between peoples; exhausted by labour, too poor to travel, they communicated with one another through thought.

Among the letters were several money orders: a Negro from the Congo had sent one franc, a Syrian from Jerusalem had sent four American dollars, a Pole called Studzinsky sent 10 zloty every three months. They were building a workers' motherland for themselves in advance, so they would have somewhere to shelter in their old age, and so their children could eventually escape and find refuge in a cold country warmed by friendship and labour.

Bozhko punctiliously invested this money in State bonds, sending the certificates by recorded delivery to their unseen owners.

After studying his mail, Bozhko would answer each letter, feeling proud and privileged to be representing the USSR. But there was no pride in what he wrote, only modesty and compassion:

> Dear, distant friend, I received your letter, everything here is going from strength to strength, the common property of the working people grows day by day, and the proletariat of the world is accumulating a vast inheritance in the form of socialism. Every day newly planted gardens are growing, new housing is being occupied, and newly invented machines are working away at speed. Different, splendid people are appearing too – only I remain as I have been, because I was born long ago and have not been able to lose the habit of being myself. In five or six years we shall have a vast quantity of cereals and all kinds of cultured comforts, and the workers from the other five-sixths of the earth, a whole billion of them, can come and live with us for ever, along with their families – and as for capitalism, let it remain empty, unless a revolution begins there. Pay attention to the Great Ocean, you live on its shore. Sometimes there are Soviet ships there – that's us. Greetings.

The African, Arratau, had told Bozhko that his wife had died; Bozhko responded with sympathy but advised him not to despair – we must save ourselves for the future, since there is no one to live on the earth but us. Better still, why didn't Arratau come straight away to the USSR? Here, among comrades, he could live more happily than with a family.

At dawn Bozhko went to sleep with the sweetness of useful exhaustion. In his sleep he dreamed he was a child. His mother was alive, it was summer in the world, there was not a breath of wind, and huge groves of trees had sprung up.

Bozhko was considered the best Stakhanovite[5] at his place of work. In addition to his main job as a geometrician, he was secretary of the wall newspaper[6] and organizer of the local branches of the Osoaviakhim[7] and the International Organization of Aid for the Fighters of the Revolution, as well as being responsible for the factory allotments and financially supporting a young girl he barely knew, paying for her to study in the school of aeronautics and thus reducing, if only by a little, the expenses of the State.

Once a month this young girl came to see Bozhko. He would hand her some sweets and give her money for her food, together with his pass for the general store, and the girl would then leave shyly. She was not quite 19 and her name was Moscow Ivanovna Chestnova. He had first met her on an autumn boulevard, at a moment of elemental sadness, and had ever since been unable to forget her.

After her visits Bozhko usually lay face down on the bed and yearned from sorrow, even though his only reason for living was universal joy. After moping for a while, he would sit down and write letters to India, Madagascar and Portugal, calling people to participate in socialism and to show solidarity with the workers on the whole of this tormented earth, and the lamp would shine on his balding head that was filled with a dream and patience.

One day Moscow Chestnova arrived as usual but did not leave straight away. Bozhko had known her for two years, but he had been too shy to gaze closely into her face, since he did not hope for anything.

Moscow was laughing; she had finished her studies at the

flying school and had brought with her some delicacies, paid for with her own money. Bozhko began to eat and drink with the young Moscow, but his heart was beating with terror, sensing the love that had long been confined in it.

When late night set in, Bozhko opened the window into dark space, and moths and mosquitoes flew inside the room, but it was so quiet everywhere that he could hear the beating of Moscow Ivanovna's heart in her large bosom; this beating was something so even, resilient and true that, had it been possible to connect the whole world to it, her heart could have regulated the course of events – even the mosquitoes and moths that alighted on the front of Moscow's blouse immediately flew away again, frightened by the hum of life in her warm and powerful body. Moscow's cheeks, enduring the pressure of her heart, had acquired a ruddiness that would last her whole life, her eyes sparkled with the clarity of happiness, her hair had been burnished by the fierceness of the heat above her head, and her body had taken on the roundness of late youth, being already on the eve of that womanly humanity that allows one human being, almost inadvertently, to begin life inside another.

Bozhko went on looking at Moscow long after the girl had fallen asleep in his room, not moving away until the new bright morning – and a drowsy, happy freshness, like health, evening and childhood, entered this tired man.

The next day Moscow invited Bozhko to the aerodrome to see how the new parachutes worked.

A small aeroplane took Moscow inside it and flew high into the age-old emptiness of the sky. When it was directly overhead, the aeroplane cut its engine, dipped forward and ejected from its underbelly a small, bright lump which began to drop breathlessly into the abyss. At the same time, flying slowly and quite close to the earth, another aeroplane had throttled back its three engines and was wanting to land. Not far above this gliding plane the solitary little airborne body hurtled helplessly down with ever-increasing speed, opened out into a flower, then filled with air and began to swing from side to side. The plane immediately started all three engines so as to move away from the parachute, but the parachute was too close, it might have been sucked into the stream of turbulence beneath the propellers, and the clever pilot once again cut the engines in order to allow the parachute freedom of movement. The parachute dropped slowly onto the surface of a wing and curled up; after a few moments a small figure walked slowly and fearlessly along the inclined wing and disappeared inside the machine.

Bozhko knew it was Moscow who had flown down out of the air. Yesterday he had heard her even, resonant heart; now he stood crying with happiness for the whole of bold humanity, regretting that for two years he had given Moscow Chestnova only 100 roubles a month and not 150.

That night, as usual, Bozhko wrote to his world of correspondents, excitedly describing the body and heart of the new human being who had overcome the deadly space of altitude.

But at dawn, his letters to humanity completed, Bozhko began to weep; it saddened him that Moscow's heart could fly through the element of air but was unable to love him. He dozed off and slept soundly until evening, quite forgetting he should have gone out to work.

In the evening there was a knock at the door and Moscow came in, looking as happy as always and with the same loud heart. Timidly, impelled by the extreme need of his feelings, Bozhko embraced Moscow, and she began to kiss him in

3

EVERY MORNING, WHEN SHE WOKE UP, MOSCOW Chestnova looked for a long time at the sunlight in the window, said in her mind, "The time of the future is coming", and got up in a state of carefree happiness that probably stemmed less from her consciousness than from health and the power of her heart. Next, Moscow would wash, marvelling at the chemistry of nature that could turn ordinary, scant food (and what filth had she not eaten in her life!) into the rosy purity and blossoming expanses of her body. While still remaining herself, Moscow Chestnova could look at herself as if she were another person and admire her own torso in the course of washing it. She understood, of course, that it was no achievement of hers, but rather the outcome of the precise work of nature and of times past. Later, as she chewed her breakfast, Moscow thought about nature: how it flowed with water and blew with wind, constantly tossing and turning its vast, patient substance, as if in the delirium of an illness . . . Nature certainly deserved compassion – it had laboured so hard in order to create man. It was like a pauper-woman who had given birth to many children and who was now stumbling about in exhaustion.

On graduating from the school of aeronautics, Moscow had been appointed a junior instructor there. Now she was teaching a group of parachutists[8] how to jump calmly out of a plane, and to retain this composure during their descent through resonant space.

Moscow herself flew with no particular sense of tension or courage; she would merely, as in her childhood, calculate the precise whereabouts of the "boundary" – where it was that technology ended and catastrophe began – and then avoid getting too close to this boundary. But the boundary was considerably more distant than people thought, and Moscow was constantly pushing it still further away.

Once she was helping to test some new parachutes which had been impregnated with a lacquer that repelled atmospheric moisture and would make it possible to jump even when it was raining. Moscow was equipped with two parachutes, the second as a precaution. She was taken up to an altitude of 2,000 metres and asked to throw herself down towards the surface of the earth, through an evening mist that had developed after long rain.

Moscow opened the door of the aeroplane and took her step into emptiness; a fierce vortex struck at her from below, as if the earth were the muzzle of a powerful blast-engine inside which air is compressed until it becomes hard and rises up as solid as a column; Moscow felt she was an empty tube, with the wind blowing right through her, and she kept her mouth constantly open so she would manage to breathe out this savage wind that was piercing right into her. Round about was a blur of mist; it was still a long way to the earth. Moscow began to swing from side to side, invisible to everyone because of the gloom – alone and free. She took out a cigarette and some matches, wanting to light up and have a smoke, but the match went out; Moscow then curled up to make a quiet, comfortable space by her bosom and immediately exploded all the matches in the box; carried by the pull of the vortex, flames seized the combustible lacquer impregnating the silk straps which linked the weight of the human being to the canopy of the parachute; these straps burnt away in less than a moment, immediately turning white-hot and scattering into ash. Moscow did not see what happened to the canopy because the wind was now burning the skin on her face, as a result of the brutal, ever-increasing speed of her fall downwards.

She flew, her cheeks red and burning, and the wind tore harshly at her body, as if it were not the wind of celestial space, but some heavy, dead substance – it was impossible to imagine that the earth would be harder and still more merciless. "So, world, this is what you're really like!" Moscow Chestnova found herself thinking as she disappeared down through the half-dark of the mist. "You're only soft so long as we don't touch you!" She pulled the ring of the reserve parachute, caught sight of the ground of the aerodrome, with its signal lights, and let out a cry of sudden torment – the opening parachute had jerked her body upwards with such force that a pain like raging tooth-ache had suddenly shot through all her bones. Two minutes later she was sitting on the grass, covered by the parachute, and she began to crawl out from under it, wiping away the tears that had been forced from her by the wind.

The first person to reach Moscow Chestnova was Arkanov, a famous pilot who in ten years of work had not bent so much as one tail-flap, never having known failure or accident.

Moscow crawled out from under the parachute to find herself a national celebrity. Arkanov and another pilot gave her their arms and took her to the common room, encouraging and complimenting her as they went along. By way of farewell Arkanov said to Moscow: "We shall be sorry to lose you, but then we seem to have lost you already. You don't understand anything at all about aviation, Moscow Ivanovna! Aviation is modesty – and you're luxury! I wish you every happiness!"

Two days later Moscow Chestnova was released from flying

duties for two years, since the atmosphere is not a circus for letting off fireworks from parachutes.

For some time newspapers and journals wrote about Moscow Chestnova's happy, youthful courage. Even the foreign press reported in full on her leap with a burning parachute and printed a beautiful photograph of the "Celestial Young Communist", but all this came to an end and Moscow never really understood what her fame was about.

She was now living on the fifth floor of a new building, in two small rooms. This building was a home to pilots, aircraft designers, engineers of all kinds, philosophers, theoretical economists and members of other professions. The windows of her flat looked out over the neighbouring city roofs while far off, in the faint, fading extremity of space, she could see thick woods and enigmatic watch-towers; at sunset some kind of strange disc would glitter there, reflecting the last of the sunlight onto the clouds and the sky. It was around 10 or 15 kilometres to this alluring land but, were she to go down onto the street, Moscow would never find her way there . . . Now that she had been dismissed from the flying school, she spent her evenings alone; she no longer went to call on Bozhko and she didn't ask her friends round. She would lean out, her stomach against the window-sill, her hair hanging down, and listen to the noise of the universal city, to its solemn energy, and to the occasional human voice that rose up from the dense and sonorous mass of moving machines; raising her head, Moscow would see the empty, destitute moon rising up into the extinguished sky and she would feel inside her a warming current of life. Her imagination was continually at work and had never yet tired – in her mind she could sense the origin of all kinds of things and she took part mentally in their existence; in her solitude she filled the whole world with her attention, watching over the flame in the street-lamps to make sure they went on shining, listening to the resounding thuds of the steam pile-drivers on the Moscow River to ensure the piles went securely down into the depths, thinking about the machines which exerted their power day and night so that light would burn in the darkness, so that the reading of books would continue, so that rye could be milled by electric motors in time for the early morning bake, and so that water could be pumped through pipes into warm shower-rooms in dance halls and the conception of a better life could take place in people's ardent and firm embraces – in the dark, in privacy, face to face, in the pure emotion of a united, doubled happiness. What Moscow Chestnova wanted was not so much to experience this life as to make sure that it came about; she wanted to stand night and day by the brake lever of the loco-motive that was taking people to meet one another; she wanted to repair water mains, to weigh out medicines for patients on pharmaceutical scales, to be a lamp that goes out just at the right moment, as people kiss, taking into itself the warmth that a moment ago had been light. She was not, however, denying her own needs – she too wanted somewhere to put her large body; she was simply postponing these needs to a more distant future, since she was patient and able to wait.

When Moscow hung out of her window during these evenings of solitude, passers-by would shout out greetings to her from down below, calling her to come and share the summer dusk with them, promising to show her the attractions of the Park of Culture and Rest and to buy her flowers and toffee creams. Moscow laughed in reply, but said nothing and stayed where she was. Later Moscow would watch from above as the roofs of the old houses in the neighbourhood began to fill up with people; whole families would make their way through attics onto these metal roofs, spreading out blankets and then lying down to sleep in the fresh air, mothers and fathers placing their children between them; courting couples would go off on their own into the ravines between roofs, somewhere between the chimney and the fire-escape, and, beneath the stars yet above the multitude of humanity, would not close their eyes until morning.

After midnight almost all the windows in sight would stop shining – the day's shock labour[9] required deep oblivion in sleep – and late cars would whisper by, not disturbing anyone with their horns. Only occasionally would these extinguished windows briefly light up again – night-shift workers were coming home, having something to eat without waking the sleepers, and then going straight to bed, while workers who had already had all their sleep – turbine operators and engine drivers, radio technicians, scientific researchers, aircraft mechanics manning early flights, and others who had been resting – were getting up to go out to work.

Moscow Chestnova would often forget to close the door of her apartment. Once she found a stranger lying on the floor, asleep on his coat. Moscow waited for her tired guest to wake up. He woke and said he was going to live right there in the corner – he had nowhere else to go. Moscow looked at the man; he was about 40, on his face lay the hardened scars of past wars, his skin had the brown, wind-beaten colour of good health and a kind heart, while a reddish moustache grew meekly over his exhausted mouth.

"I wouldn't have come in without asking, my shaggy beauty," said her unknown guest, "but a body needs peace, and there just isn't anywhere . . . I shan't get in your way – you can pretend

I don't exist, that I'm just an extra table. There won't be sight nor sound nor smell of me."

Moscow asked him who he was, and her guest explained everything about himself in detail, showing her his documents.

"What do you expect?" said the man who had moved in. "I'm an ordinary man, everything about me is in order."

He turned out to be from Yelets and his job was weighing out firewood in a warehouse. And Moscow could not bring herself to postpone communism because of a housing shortage and her right to additional space; she said nothing and gave her lodger a pillow and a blanket. The lodger settled in; at night he would get up, then tiptoe to the bed of the sleeping Moscow in order to pull her blanket back over her because she was always tossing and turning, throwing the bed-clothes off and getting cold. In the morning he never used the toilet in the apartment, not wanting to burden it with his filth and make a noise with the water; he would go instead to the public toilet in the yard below. After a few days of life in her apartment, this weigher of wood was already mending the heels on Moscow's worn-out shoes, secretly brushing off bits of dirt that had stuck to her autumn coat, and putting the kettle on in joyous anticipation of his landlady's awakening. At first Moscow scolded the weigher for being fawning, but after a while, to put an end to this slavery, she introduced a regime of socialist self-sufficiency, darning her lodger's socks and even shaving his stubble with a safety razor.

Soon after this the Komsomol[10] organization allocated Moscow a temporary job in the regional military enlistment office; her task would be to liquidate registration irregularities.

4

ONE DAY A PALE THIN MAN, A RESERVIST,[11] WAS STANDING in the corridor of the enlistment office, his military registration book in his hand. It seemed to him that the office had the same smell as places of prolonged confinement – the lifeless smell of a pining human body that consciously chooses to act modestly and thriftily, so as not to awaken the fading desire for a distant life and vainly torture itself with the ache of despair. The insignificance of the staff, the impersonally ideological furnishings, which had been provided from a meagre budget – all this promised the visitor the unsympathetic treatment that comes from a cruel or impoverished heart.

The reservist waited by one of the windows for the clerk to finish reading a poem in her book; he believed that poems make everyone kinder – in the youth of his life he too had read books until midnight, and afterwards had felt sad and calm. The clerk finished the poem and began to re-register the reservist, expressing her astonishment that, according to the registration form, this man had served in neither the White nor the Red Army, had not undergone the universal military training, had never reported to any recruitment centres, had never been a member of any territorial units or taken part in Osoaviakhim marches, and was now three years late in reporting to be re-registered. It was unclear how and in what kind of silence this reservist, with his old-style military registration book, had managed to hide from the vigilance of the house management committees.

The military clerk looked at the reservist. In front of her, behind the partition that protected the calm of the institution from visitors, stood a man whose emaciated face was covered by the lines of a life of dreariness and by bleak traces of weakness and suffering; the reservist's clothes were as worn as the skin on his face and they kept the man warm only by means of the long-lasting filth that had eaten its way into the decrepitude of the cloth. He was watching the clerk with timid cunning, not expecting compassion, and often looking down and closing his eyes completely so as to see darkness rather than life; for a moment he would imagine the clouds in the sky – he loved them because they had nothing to do with him and he was a stranger to them.

Happening to look into the depths of the office, the reservist gave a start of surprise; two clear eyes were watching him from beneath concentrated eyebrows, not holding any threat. Somewhere or other the reservist had often seen eyes like these – eyes that were attentive and pure – and he had always blinked when he met their gaze. "This is the real Red Army!" he thought with wistful shame. "Lord! Why have I wasted my whole life just keeping myself going?" The reservist had never expected anything from institutions but horror, exhaustion and long-suffering dreariness, but now he saw in the distance a human being who was thinking about him with compassion.

The "Red Army" got to its feet, proving to be a woman, and went up to the reservist. He was frightened by the charm and power of her face, but out of pity for his heart, which might start vainly aching with love, he turned away from this clerk. Moscow Chestnova, the woman who had walked up to him, took his registration book and fined him 50 roubles for infringement of the registration law.

"I haven't got any money," said the reservist. "I'd rather pay in kind somehow."

"What do you mean?" asked Moscow.

"I don't know," said the reservist quietly. "I don't live very well."

Moscow took him by the hand and led him to her desk.

"Why don't you live very well?" she asked. "Is there anything you want?"

The reservist was unable to answer; this Red Army clerk smelt of soap and sweat, and also of some sweet life unknown to his heart – a heart that was used to hiding away in its own solitude, its own barely smouldering warmth. He bowed his head and began to cry because things were so miserable for him, and Moscow Chestnova let go of his hand in bewilderment. The reservist stood there for a while and then, glad that he was not being detained, disappeared to his unknown dwelling, to keep himself going one way or another up to the edge of the grave, without registration or danger.

But Moscow found his address on the re-registration form and, some time later, went to call on him.

She wandered for a long time in the depths of the Bauman district before she found the small housing co-operative where the reservist lived. This was a building with an incompetent management committee, and with accounts that were in deficit; the walls had not been painted for years, and the grim, empty yard, where even the stones were worn down from the games of children, had long been in need of proper attention.

Moscow felt sad as she followed the walls of the building, then made her way down dimly lit corridors; it was as though she had been hurt by someone or as though she herself were to blame for the careless, unhappy lives of other people. When she emerged on the other side of the building, which faced a long, blank fence, she saw a stone porch, with an iron awning and an electric lamp shining above it. She listened closely to the noise in the surrounding air: behind the fence, planks of wood were being thrown to the ground and she could hear spades cutting into the earth; beside the iron awning was a hatless, bald man, standing there on his own and playing a mazurka on the fiddle. Lying on a stone slab was the musician's hat; it had lived, on his head, through long misfortunes of every kind; once it had covered a youthful head of hair, and now it was collecting money for the sustenance of old age, for the support of a feeble consciousness in a bare, decrepit head.

Moscow put a rouble in this hat and asked the man to play her some Beethoven. Without saying a word, the musician played on until he'd finished the mazurka and only then began some Beethoven. Moscow stood opposite the fiddler like a peasant woman, her feet wide apart and her face full of grief from the agitated yearning around her heart. The whole world around her suddenly became harsh and intransigent – it was composed entirely of hard and heavy objects, and a harsh, dark force was acting with such malice that it fell into despair and began to cry with an emaciated human voice, a voice on the edge of its own silence. Now once again this force was rising up from its iron world and, with the speed of a howl, was smashing to pieces some enemy of its own, some cold bureaucratic enemy that occupied all infinity with its dead torso. This music was losing all melody and turning into a strident cry of attack, yet it still had the rhythm of an ordinary human heart and was as simple as a feat that is beyond one's strength but which one performs out of vital need.

The musician looked at Moscow indifferently and without paying attention to her, not attracted by any of her charms – as an artist, he always felt within his soul some better and more manly charm that drew his will onward, beyond ordinary pleasure, and he preferred this charm to anything visible. Towards the end of the piece, tears came from the fiddler's eyes. He was exhausted by living and, above all, he had failed, in his own life, to live up to the music; instead of meeting his early death beneath the walls of an insuperable enemy, he was standing in the deserted yard of a housing co-operative, old, poor and alive, with the last dream of a heroic world still drifting through his exhausted mind. Opposite, on the other side of the fence, they were building a medical institute that would search for longevity and immortality, but the old musician was unable to understand that this construction was a continuation of Beethoven's music, and Moscow Chestnova did not know what was being built there. Any music, provided it was great and humane, reminded Moscow of the proletariat, of the dark man with the burning torch who had run into the night of the Revolution, and of her own self, and she listened to it as though it were both the Leader's speech and her own words – words she was always meaning to say but had never said out loud.

On the main door hung a plywood board with the inscription: "Housing Co-operative Administration and House Management Committee". Moscow went inside, to find out the number of the reservist's room – on the registration form he had given only the number of the building.

The co-operative office was down a wooden corridor. On each side, no doubt, lived families with many children, and these children were now crying out in hurt and frustration as they divided up the food they had been given for supper. Inside the corridor tenants were standing and talking about every subject under the sun: food supplies, repairs to the toilets in the yard, the coming war, the stratosphere, and the death of the local laundry-woman, who had been deaf and insane. The walls of the corridor were hung with posters from the Savings Bank Board, posters from the International Organization of Aid for the Fighters of the Revolution,[12] posters that explained the rules of baby care or that bore a picture of a man shaped like the letter Я, one of his legs cut short by a road accident, and other images of life, welfare and misfortune. Around five o'clock in the evening, straight after work, people would gather in this wooden corridor and then stand about on their feet, thinking and talking, right up until midnight, only occasionally asking the house management committee for some letter of reference. Moscow Chestnova was astonished; she could not understand why people clung to the co-operative, to the office, to letters of reference, to the local needs of a small happiness, to wearing themselves out in trivialities, when the city had world-class theatres and there were still eternal enigmas of suffering to be resolved in life, and when, no further off than the main door, a fiddler was playing splendid music that nobody heard.

The elderly house-manager, who was working in the noise of people, amidst smoke and all kinds of questions, gave Moscow precise details about everything to do with the reservist: he lived in the first-floor corridor system, in room number four, he was a category three pensioner,[13] the housing-co-operative volunteer activists had visited him many times and attempted to persuade him of the urgent necessity of his re-registering himself and formally clarifying his position with regard to army service. The reservist had been promising to do all this for several years, saying he would start the next morning and devote the whole day to official requirements, and yet, for some senseless reason, he had still not carried out these promises. Six months ago the house manager had visited the reservist to discuss these matters himself; he had exhorted the reservist for three hours, comparing his melancholy and boredom to a kind of physical uncleanliness – it was as if he didn't wash or brush his teeth. In sum, he was bringing shame on himself, with the intention of denigrating Soviet man.

"I really don't know what to do with him," said the house manager. "There's no one else like him in the entire co-operative."

"What does he actually do?" asked Moscow.

"I've already told you – he's a category three pensioner, he gets 45 roubles a month. Oh yes, and he's also a member of the volunteer militia, he goes and stands at a tram stop, fines a few people and then comes back to his room."

Moscow felt saddened by the life of such a man, and said, "How wrong it all is!"

The house manager entirely agreed: "There's nothing about him that isn't wrong! In summer he often goes to the Park of Culture and Rest – but goodness knows why! He never listens to the band or goes to see the attractions – he just sits himself down by the militia post and spends the whole day there. Sometimes he'll talk a little, sometimes he'll go off and do some errand they've given him. He likes administrative work – he's a good volunteer."

"Is he married?" asked Moscow.

"No, he's undefined . . . Officially he's a bachelor, but for years now he's been quietly spending all his nights with women. In principle that's his business, it's no concern of the housing co-operative. But the trouble is these women have no culture, they're worthless – there's never been anyone like you before. I'd stay away from him – he's a wretch of a man."

Moscow left the management office. As before, the musician was standing by the entrance, but he was no longer playing anything, just listening in silence to something from out of the night. A distant glow was flickering above the centre of the city, rippling through fast-moving clouds; and the enormous sky, packed with darkness, was suddenly yet repeatedly being opened up by quick sharp lights that flashed from the tram-wires. A choir of young women was singing in a nearby club for local transport workers, carrying their own lives, through the power of inspiration, into the distant realms of the future. Moscow went into this club, and sang and danced there until the master of ceremonies put out the lights, wanting the young people to get some rest. Moscow then went to sleep on a ply-wood prop somewhere behind the stage; in her girlish way she was hugging her temporary companion, a young woman as tired and happy as she was herself.

5

SAMBIKIN'S ECONOMY WITH TIME MADE HIM UNTIDY
and slovenly, and the world's external matter felt to him like
an irritation of his own skin. Day and night he followed the
world-wide current of events, and his mind lived in a terror of
responsibility for the entire senseless fate of physical substance.

At night Sambikin took a long time to fall asleep, because he
was imagining the labour, now lit by electricity, that was in
progress on Soviet land. He saw structures, densely equipped
with scaffolding, where unsleeping people came and went as
they fastened down young boards made from fresh timber so
as to be able to remain up there, high up, where the wind blows
and from where night, in the form of the last remnant of the
evening glow, can be seen moving along the edge of the world.
Sambikin would clasp his hands in impatience and joy, then
suddenly fall into thought in the darkness, forgetting to blink
for half-an-hour at a time. He knew that thousands of young
engineers, who had just finished their shifts, were also unable
to sleep, and were agitatedly tossing and turning in hostels and
new buildings all over the flat plains of the country, while others,
who had only that moment lain down to rest, were already
muttering to themselves and gradually pulling their clothes back
on again, wanting to go back to the building site because their
minds were being tormented by some detail, forgotten about
during the day, which threatened nocturnal disaster.

Sambikin would get out of bed, turn on the light and walk
about in anxiety, wanting to start some activity straight away.
He would turn on the radio but would find that music was no

longer playing, while space was humming in its anxiety, like a deserted road that asks to be walked along. Then Sambikin would phone the institute clinic, ask if there were any urgent operations, and offer to assist. He was told that there was one. A little boy had been brought in with a tumour on his head; it was growing from minute to minute, and his consciousness was darkening.

Sambikin ran out onto the Moscow street; the trams were no longer running, and the high heels of women on their way back from theatres and laboratories, or from visiting people they loved, were clacking along the asphalt pavements. Working his long legs, Sambikin ran quickly to the Bauman district, where an experimental medical institute was being constructed. It had not yet been fully equipped, and only two departments – surgery and casualty – were functioning. The institute yard was heaped with boards, pipes, trolleys and crates of scientific instruments; the child-high fence, which separated the buildings from some kind of apartment block, had begun to wilt and was leaning right over.

In this yard Sambikin suddenly heard a plaintive music which touched his heart not so much through its melody as through some vague memory of something that had been lived through and then left behind in oblivion. He listened intently for a minute; the music was playing on the other side of the meagre fence. He climbed onto this fence and saw a bald, aged fiddler playing on his own, at two o'clock in the morning. Sambikin read the sign over the main door of the building outside which the fiddler was playing: "Housing Co-operative Administration and House Management Committee". He took out a rouble and wanted to give it to the musician for his work, but the fiddler refused it. He said he was playing for himself now, because he felt melancholy and full of *toskà*; he was unable to go to sleep until dawn, and that was still a long way off . . .

Two oxygen cylinders had been hung outside the smaller of the operating theatres, and the senior duty nurse was standing there. At the end of the corridor, in a separate cubicle whose front wall was made entirely of glass, the sick child was being prepared for the operation; two nurses were rapidly shaving his head. Behind the boy's left ear was a ball, half the size of his head and filled with hot brown pus and blood, and this ball looked like a second malign head that was sucking out the exhausted life of the child. The child was sitting up in bed, unable to sleep; he was about seven years old. He was staring with empty, sleeping eyes, and lifting his hands in the air a little when his heart gasped with pain; he was in torment and expected no mercy.

Sambikin immediately, and with exact sensation, experienced the child's illness in his own vivid consciousness, and he rubbed the skin behind his left ear, looking for a spherical swelling, a second mindless head packed with deadly pus. Then he went to get ready for the operation.

As he got changed, he continued to think about the boy. He heard a noise in his left ear – it was the pus in the boy's head, chemically eroding and corroding the last plate of bone that protected his brain. The mist of death was already spreading through the boy's mind, life was still clinging on in the shelter of this film of bone, but it was now only a fraction of a millimetre thick and the weakening bone was vibrating beneath the pressure of the pus.

"What does he see in his consciousness now?" Sambikin was asking himself. "He sees dreams that protect him from horror. Two nurses are shaving his head, but what he sees is two mothers washing him in the bath. And the only thing that frightens him is: why has he got two mothers? He sees his favourite cat, that lives in his room at home, and now this cat's sunk its claws into his head."

In came the old surgeon, the man Sambikin was to assist. The old man was ready, and he beckoned to his assistant. Sambikin was not yet allowed to operate on his own; he was 27 years old and in his second year of working as an assistant surgeon.

All the sounds in the surgical clinic were scrupulously blotted out, and communication was now effected through coloured lights. Three lamps of different colours came on in the room of the doctor on duty, and a number of actions were performed almost noiselessly: a low trolley moved on rubber wheels down the cork floor of the corridor and took the patient away to the operating theatre; the electrician switched the lights over to the institute's own storage batteries, so light would no longer depend upon the vicissitudes of the city grid, and then turned on a machine which pumped ozone-enriched air into the operating theatre; the door of the theatre opened without a sound, and a cool, fragrant breeze blew into the face of the sick child from a special apparatus. This brought the boy sedation and he smiled, freed from the last traces of suffering.

"Mummy, I'm ever so ill. They're going to cut me now, but I'm not hurting at all!" he said, and then became helpless and estranged from himself. Life seemed to leave him, concentrating instead in the sad, distant imagination of dreams. He saw objects – the entire sum of his experience. The objects rushed past him and he recognized them: here was a forgotten nail he had held in his hands long ago, now the nail had rusted and grown old; here – a small black dog he had once played with in the yard, now it was lying dead in the rubbish, with a

33

broken glass jar on its head; here – an iron roof on a low shed, he had climbed up there so he could look at the world from high up, now the roof was empty and the iron was missing him, it was a long time since he'd been there; it was summer, his mother's shadow lay on the ground, police were marching by, but their band was playing too softly to be heard . . .

The old surgeon suggested Sambikin carry out the operation – he himself would assist.

"Let's start!" said the old man, in the bright, remote silence of the theatre.

Sambikin took a keen and gleaming instrument and entered with it into what is the essence of all things – the human body. A sharp, instantaneous arrow left the boy's mind, just behind his eyes, ran through his body – Sambikin was following the arrow with his imagination – and struck the boy in the heart; the boy shuddered, every object that had ever known him began to cry for him, and the dream of his memories vanished. Life sank even lower, smouldering with a dark and simple warmth as it waited patiently. With his hands Sambikin could feel the boy's body growing still hotter, and he worked fast. He was draining pus from the now wide-open integuments of the head and penetrating into the bone, searching for the primary seats of infection.

"Gently, take your time," the old surgeon was saying. Then he turned to the nurse and asked: "What's the pulse?"

"It's arrhythmic, doctor," said the nurse. "Sometimes it disappears completely."

"Never mind – the momentum of the heart is considerable. It'll right itself."

"Hold his head," Sambikin ordered the nurses. He was now starting to clean out the areas of bone in whose cavities the pus was concealed.

His instruments clinked, as if he were working cold metal. Stroke by stroke – a deep cut here, a more shallow cut there – Sambikin was feeling his way, guided by the precise sense of art. His big eyes had gone glassy from lack of moisture – there was no time to blink – and his pale cheeks had turned dark from the force of the blood coming to his help from the depths of his heart. As he picked out the sections of bone, Sambikin examined them by the light of the reflector; he sniffed them and squeezed them so as to get to know them better, and then handed them over to the senior surgeon, who threw them indifferently into a container.

The brain was getting closer; as he removed pieces of bone from the skull, Sambikin was now studying them under a microscope and still finding nests of streptococci. In some parts of the child's head Sambikin had already reached the last membrane of bone guarding the brain, and he began to scrape the deadly grey film from its surface. His hands acted as if thinking for themselves, calculating each possibility of movement. As he progressed, the streptococci diminished in number, but Sambikin then moved over to extremely powerful microscopes which showed that the pus-generating bodies, though rapidly growing fewer, were still not disappearing entirely. He remembered the well-known mathematical equation expressing the distribution of heat along a bar of infinite length, and brought the operation to a close.

"Pack the wound and bandage it!" he ordered, for the complete destruction of the streptococci would entail cutting to pieces not only the whole of the patient's head but also his entire body right down to his toenails.

Sambikin could see clearly that the patient's body, hot, defenceless and wide-open, with its thousands of cut blood-vessels, was greedily absorbing streptococci from everywhere –

from the air and, above all, from his own instruments, which it was impossible to sterilize absolutely. Hospitals should have changed over long ago to an electrical surgery that entered body and bones with the pure and instantaneous blue flame of an electric arc – then everything that brought death would be destroyed, and any new streptococci that entered a wound would find a burnt-out desert, not an environment that would nourish them.

"Finished!" said Sambikin.

The nurses were already bandaging the patient's head. They turned him over, his face towards the doctors.

The warmth of life, beating out from within, passed in pink bands across the child's pale face and was quickly washed away; it reappeared only to fade again. His eyes were almost open and had become so dry that the substance of the retina had grown slightly wrinkled.

"He's dead!" said the old doctor.

"Not yet," Sambikin answered, and kissed the child on his pale lips. "He'll live. Give him a little oxygen. And nothing to drink until morning."

On his way out from the clinic, Sambikin came across a convulsively trembling woman – the child's mother. She had not been allowed in because of the rules and it being late at night. Sambikin nodded to her and ordered her to be admitted to her son.

Morning was brightening. Sambikin looked across the fence to the neighbouring housing co-operative; everything was deserted, the fiddler had gone away to sleep. A man of humble appearance came out of the door, together with a wrinkled woman who had been worn out by years and hardship. Her companion was eloquently declaring his love; Sambikin couldn't help but listen more closely to his voice – he could hear a dark, chesty sorrow in it, and that made it touching, even though the man's words were stupid and trite.

"But if there's a war, you'll drop me," the woman was timidly objecting.

"Me? Certainly not! I'm last category, a reservist, I'm almost nothing . . . Let's go and lie down a bit behind the shed – my soul's aching again."

"Didn't you get enough of loving me when we were in the room?" the woman asked in happy surprise.

"Not quite enough," said the reservist lover. "My heart's still aching, it hasn't cooled down yet."

"A right young Hamlet!" said the woman with a smile. "Nothing stops him!"

She now felt proud that men liked her and were attracted by her. Hunched from the morning cold beneath his worn-out, tired coat, the reservist hurried off arm in arm with the woman, evidently eager to get shot of everything as soon as he possibly could.

Sambikin set off through the city. It felt strange and even sad to see the empty tram stops and the deserted black route-numbers on their white signs – along with the pavements, the tramway poles, and the electric clock on the square, they were yearning for crowds of people.

As was his way, Sambikin began to ponder the life of matter – the life of his own self; it was as if he were a laboratory animal, the part of the world he had been allocated so that he could investigate the entirety of everything, in all its obscurity.

He thought constantly and without interruption; if he stopped thinking, his soul immediately began to ache, and he would get back to work inside his head, imagining the world in order to transform it. At night he dreamed of his destroyed thoughts and tossed and turned in bed to no avail, trying to recall their daytime sequence; then he would feel distressed and would wake up, glad of the morning light and restored clarity of mind. His body was long and dried-up, kind and big, and it always lived and breathed noisily, as if this man were greedy; he wanted constantly to eat and drink, and his huge face had the look of a saddened animal, except that the nose was so very big, so alien even to this huge face, that it imparted meekness to the entire expression of his character.

It was already daylight when Sambikin got home; the great summer morning was burning in the sky with such power that its light seemed to be thundering. He phoned the institute and was told that the boy he had operated on was sleeping soundly, that his temperature was falling and that his mother had gone to sleep in the other bed. After going over in his mind all the routine problems, and everything concerning the operation, Sambikin began to sense his melancholy, now empty heart – once more he needed to act, in order to find himself a problem to contemplate and thus silence the obscure, hungering cry of conscience in his soul. He slept little – except after prolonged work, in gratitude for which his dreams would leave him alone. But at present he was not being active enough, his reason had not been able to tire itself out in his head and it rejected sleep, wanting to go on working. After pacing helplessly about the room, Sambikin went into the bathroom; he undressed and looked in astonishment at his young man's body, then muttered something and got into the cold water. The water pacified him, but he immediately realized how much a human being was still a poorly constructed, homespun creature – no more than a vague embryo, or blueprint, of something more authentic – and how much work was needed in order for this embryo to develop into the soaring, lofty image that lies buried in our dreams.

6

THAT EVENING, IN THE LOCAL KOMSOMOL CLUB, THERE
was a gathering of young scientists, engineers, pilots, doctors,
teachers, performing artists, musicians and workers from the
new factories. No one was over the age of 27, yet each of them
was already known throughout the new world of their motherland – and this early fame made them all feel a slight shame,
which got in the way of their lives. The men and women
who worked at the club, who were older and who had wasted
their lives and talent during the unhappy bourgeois times, let
out secret sighs of inner impoverishment as they arranged the
furnishings in the two halls, setting up one for a formal meeting
and the other for conversing and dining.

Among the first to arrive were Selin – a 24-year-old engineer–
and Kuzmina – a pianist and Komsomol member who was
constantly deep in thought from the imagination of music.

"Let's get ourselves a bite to eat!" said Selin.

"Yes, let's!" Kuzmina agreed.

They went over to the bar. Selin, a pink-cheeked and hearty
eater, immediately consumed eight pieces of bread and salami,
while Kuzmina took only two pastries; it was music she lived
for, not the digestion of food.

"Selin, why do you eat such a lot?" asked Kuzmina. "It may
be good for you, but it's an embarrassment to watch!"

Selin had an indignant way of eating; he chewed as if he were
ploughing, his trusty jaws labouring persistently and with zeal.

After a while, ten more people arrived together: Golovach the
explorer; the mechanical engineer Semyon Sartorius; two girls,

who were friends, both of them hydraulic engineers; Levchenko the composer; Sitsylin the astronomer; Vechkin the aviation meteorologist; Muldbauer the designer of high-altitude aircraft; and the electrical engineer Gunkin, with his wife. Then came the sound of other voices, and some more people arrived. They all knew one another – through work, through meeting socially, or through hearsay.

While they waited for the meeting to begin, they each devoted themselves to their particular pleasure: to friendship, to food, to questions about unresolved problems, or to music and dancing. Kuzmina found a small room with a new grand piano, and with pleasure began playing Beethoven's Ninth – all the movements, one after another, from memory. Her heart was wrung by the music's inspired thought and deep freedom, as well as by egotistical sorrow at not being able to compose like that herself. Gunkin the electrical engineer listened to Kuzmina and thought about the high frequencies of electricity that sweep through the universe, and about the emptiness of the high, terrible world that sucks all human consciousness into itself. Muldbauer saw in the music a representation of the distant, weightless countries of the air, countries of the black sky and the unflickering sun that hangs there with the dead incandescence of its light, countries that lie far from the warm and dimly green earth and that mark the beginning of the real, serious cosmos begins: mute space, lit up now and again by stars signalling that the path there has long been open and free. Yes, better to put an end straight away to the bothersome conflicts of the earth; let Stalin himself, let wise old Stalin, direct the velocity and thrust of human history beyond the bounds of the earth's gravity – to the great edification of the earth, to the great edification of reason itself through the courage of an act it has long been destined to perform.

Soon afterwards Moscow Chestnova arrived too, smiling quietly from the joy of seeing her comrades and hearing music that excited her life towards the fulfilment of a higher fate.

Last of all came the surgeon Sambikin; he had come straight from the clinic, where he had been changing the bandages on the sick boy. He arrived feeling burdened by the sorrow of the construction of the human body, which squeezes within its bones far more suffering and death than life and movement. And he found it strange to be feeling well now, in the tension of his concerns and responsibilities. His whole mind was filled with thought, his heart was beating calmly and truly, he had no need of any better happiness – yet, at the same time, consciousness of his secret pleasure made him feel ashamed. He was about to leave the club, to go to the Institute and do some work during the night on his research into death, when suddenly he saw Moscow Chestnova passing by. The elusive charm of her appearance surprised Sambikin; concealed behind the modesty and even timidity of her face, he could see power and luminous inspiration.

A bell rang, announcing the start of the meeting. Everyone left the room; only Moscow stayed behind, pulling one of her stockings tight. When she had done this, she saw that Sambikin was on his own, and was looking at her. Out of awkwardness and embarrassment – that they should live in the same world, be devoted to the same cause, and yet not be acquainted – she nodded to him. Sambikin walked over to her, and together they went through to listen to the meeting.

They sat down side by side and, amid the speeches, amid the toasts and glory, Sambikin clearly heard the pulsing of Moscow's heart in her breast. "Why is your heart knocking like that? I can hear it!" he whispered into her ear.

"It wants to fly, that's what makes it beat," Moscow whispered back to Sambikin with a smile. "I'm a parachutist!"

"In long-ago, now perished millennia, the human body did fly," thought Sambikin. "The human ribcage represents folded wings."

He touched his head, which felt warm; there too something was beating its wings, wanting to fly out from the cell of a dark, lonely confinement.

After the meeting, it was time for the communal dinner and the entertainments. But first, before they sat down together at the shared table, the young guests dispersed through the many rooms.

Sartorius the mechanical engineer asked Moscow Chestnova to dance, and she began to whirl about with him, studying with curiosity the great round face of this famous inventor in the field of precision industry, this engineer and designer of world-wide importance. Sartorius held Moscow tightly, danced heavily and smiled timidly, revealing his compressed feelings for her. Moscow, for her part, looked at him as if she were in love – she was always quick to abandon herself to her feelings, not resorting to the feminine policy of indifference. She liked this dull man who was shorter than her, whose face was kind and morose, and who, unable to contend with his heart, had undertaken an act of what for him was extreme boldness: he had gone up to a woman and asked her to dance. Soon, however, he began to seem bored; his hands had grown used to the warmth of Moscow's body, which was hot beneath her light dress, and he began to mutter something. At this, Moscow immediately took offence.

"He comes and asks me to dance, he takes me in his arms, and then he thinks about something completely different!" she said out loud.

"It's nothing," answered Sartorius.

"What's nothing? You can tell me right now!" Moscow said with a frown, and stopped dancing.

Sambikin hurtled past, creating a wind; he too was dancing, having paired up with some Komsomol girl of great prettiness. Moscow smiled at him: "You're dancing too! How come? You are a surprise!"

"One should live on all fronts!" Sambikin informed her without pausing.

"And are you enjoying it?" Moscow shouted after him.

"No, I'm pretending!" Sambikin answered. "I was speaking theoretically."

The pretty Komsomol girl was offended and immediately left Sambikin, who began to laugh.

"Well go on then! Tell me!" Moscow said to Sartorius with mock seriousness.

"Is she stupid?" thought Sartorius. "What a shame!" At this moment Vechkin, the meteorologist, came up to him, followed by Sambikin, and Sartorius was unable to say anything to Moscow in reply. An hour passed before they met again at the communal table.

The large table had been laid for 50 people. Every half-metre there were flowers, looking pensive because of their beauty and giving off a posthumous fragrance. The wives of the designers, and the young women engineers, were dressed in the best silk of the Republic – the government liked to adorn its best people. Moscow Chestnova was wearing her tea-rose dress, which weighed only ten grams and had been sewn with such skill that even the pulsing of her blood vessels was revealed by the rippling of the silk. All the men, even the untidy Sambikin and the shaggy, melancholy Vechkin, had come in suits that were simple but expensive, made from the finest material; to dress badly and in slovenly fashion would have been to reproach with poverty the country that had nourished everyone present and dressed them with her choicest goods, herself thriving on their youthful strength and drive, on their talent and labour.

Outside the open door, on the balcony, a small Komsomol band was playing short pieces. The spacious air of the night came through this balcony door and into the hall, and the flowers on the long table breathed and gave off a stronger smell, feeling that they were alive again in the earth they had lost. The ancient city was full of clamour and light, like a construction site; now and again the voice and laughter of a passer-by would be carried in from the street, and Moscow Chestnova would feel like going outside and inviting everybody to join them: after all, socialism was dawning! At times she felt so good that she wanted somehow to leave herself behind, to leave her body and its dress, and become someone else – Gunkin's wife, Sambikin, the reservist, Sartorius, or a woman working on a collective farm in the Ukraine.

Chandeliers from the "ElectroDevice" factory cast a pale and tender energy over the people and the rich furnishings; preliminary light snacks stood on the table while the main supper was kept warm far off on the kitchen ranges.

The assembled company, who were all beautiful either from nature or from animation and unfinished youth, took a long time to sit down at the table, looking for the best people to sit beside, though what they really wanted was to sit next to everyone at once.

When they finally sat down, all 30 of them, their inner resources of life were excited by one another's company and began to multiply, and among them was born the shared genius of vital sincerity and of happy rivalry in intellectual friendship. But their finely tuned sense of relationship, acquired in a difficult, technological culture where victory is not to be won by ambiguous games – this sense of right conduct allowed no place for stupidity, sentimentality or conceit. They all knew, or guessed at, the sullen dimensions of nature, the extensiveness of history, the length of future time and the true scale of their own powers; they were rational and practical people, not to be seduced by empty delusion.

Moscow Chestnova was wilder, more impatient than the others. Without waiting for anyone else, she had drunk a glass of wine, and now she was flushed – from joy and from being unused to drinking. Sartorius noticed this and smiled at her with his broad, inexact face that made one think of some place in the country. His father's surname was not Sartorius but Chewbeard, and his peasant mother had carried him in her innards beside warm, well-chewed rye bread.

Sambikin was also observing Moscow, and puzzling over her: should he love her or not? All in all, she was good-looking, and she belonged to nobody, but how much thought and feeling would he have to drive out of his body and heart so as to make room there for affection for this woman? And anyway Moscow would not be faithful to him; she would never be able to exchange all the noise of life for the whisper of a single human being.

"No!" Sambikin decided once and for all. "I won't love her – and I can't! All the more so since I'd end up somehow damaging her body, and that would be sad. And I'd have to lie, day and night, about how splendid I am. I don't want to, it's too difficult!" He forgot himself in the flow of his thoughts, the other guests slipping from his consciousness. These other guests, although the dishes before them were both plentiful and tasty, were all eating little and slowly, chary of eating precious food that the workers on the collective farms had won for them, through labour and patience, during the terrible struggle with nature and the class enemy. Only Moscow Chestnova forgot herself, eating and drinking like some predatory creature. She said all kinds of foolish things, teased Sartorius and felt shame stealing into her heart from her vulgar, lying mind that was sadly aware of its shameful state. Nobody was rude to Moscow or tried to stop her, and finally she exhausted her strength and fell silent of her own accord. Sambikin knew that foolishness was a natural expression of wandering feelings that have not yet found their goal and passion, while Sartorius took delight in Moscow regardless of her behaviour; he already loved her as if she were a living truth, and through his joy he saw her unclearly and inaccurately.

Amid a hubbub of people and an evening that was already late, Viktor Vasilievich Bozhko quietly entered the hall and sat down on a couch by the wall, not wanting to be noticed. He caught sight of Moscow Chestnova, now flushed and merry, and trembled from fear. Some learned young man went over to her and sang:

> Your face is pale,
> You don't walk straight,
> My drunken love,
> My friend, my fate.

At this, Moscow covered her face with her hands, either weeping or suddenly ashamed of herself. Sartorius was at that moment arguing with Vechkin and Muldbauer, attempting to prove that man as a creature of class will be superseded on earth by an impassioned and technological being who will experience the whole world in a practical way, through work. The ancients, the people who began history, were also technological beings; the cities, ports and labyrinths of Greece, even Mount Olympus itself, were constructed by Cyclops, one-eyed workers – the ancient aristocrats had gouged out their other eye as a sign that this was the proletariat, doomed to build countries, dwellings for the gods and ships for the seas, and that there is no escape for the one-eyed. Three or four thousand years had gone by – a hundred generations – and the descendants of these Cyclops had emerged from the dark of the historical labyrinth into the light of nature; they had retained one sixth of the earth, and all the rest of the earth lived solely in expectation of their coming. Even the god Zeus had probably been a Cyclops, the very last Cyclops; his work had been to heap up the hill of Olympus, and he had lived in a hut up above and had survived in the memory of the ancient aristocratic tribe. For the bourgeoisie of those ancient times had not been stupid; it had elevated great workers who died to the rank of gods. Being unable to understand creativity without pleasure, it was secretly astonished that these dead could quietly have possessed the highest power of all – the capacity for labour – as well as technology – which was the soul of labour.

Sartorius rose to his feet and took up a cup of wine. A short man, carried away by intellectual imagination, and with an ordinary face that was warmed by life, he was happy and attractive. Moscow Chestnova gazed at him and decided that one day they must kiss. In the midst of his now silent comrades he pronounced: "Let us drink to the nameless Cyclops, to the memory of all our exhausted fathers who have perished, and to technology – the true soul of mankind!"

They all drank together, and the musicians played an old song, a setting of some lines of Yazykov:[14]

> Beyond the wall of stormy weather,
> Lies a country that is blessed,
> Where the heavens never darken,
> Where all is quietness and rest.

Bozhko sat there submissively and inconspicuously. He felt more joy than any of the other guests; he knew that the stormy weather was passing and that the country of the blessed lay outside the window, lit by stars and electricity. He loved this country in a silent and parsimonious fashion, picking up every crumb of its riches that fell to the ground, in order that the country should survive in its entirety.

A lavish main course was brought in. Carefully the guests began to taste it, but Semyon Sartorius could no longer eat or drink anything. An agony of love for Moscow Chestnova had taken hold of all his body and heart, and he had to open his mouth and make an effort to breathe, as if he felt tight in the chest. From some way away Moscow was smiling enigmatically; her mysterious life reached Sartorius in the form of warmth and alarm, while her keen eyes were looking at him inattentively, as though he were some everyday fact. "What a bitch life is!" Sartorius said to himself, as he grasped what was happening to him. "There's nothing left for me now except foolishness and personal happiness."

The city night shone in the darkness outside, sustained by the tension of distant machines; warmed by millions of people, the excited air entered Sartorius's heart in the form of longing and despair. He went out onto the balcony, glanced at the stars and whispered old words he had heard and remembered: "My God!"

Sambikin was still sitting at the table, not touching the food; his own thoughts had led him far beyond the next morning and he was trying confusedly, as if through a sea-fog, to glimpse the immortality to come. He wanted to obtain a long-lasting power of life, maybe an eternity of it, from the corpses of beings who had perished. A few years back, while digging about inside dead human bodies, he had taken fine sections from their hearts, brains and organs of sexual secretion. Sambikin had studied these sections under the microscope and had seen faint traces of some unknown substance. Later, testing these almost extinguished traces for chemical reactivity, electrical conductivity and photosensitivity, he had discovered that this unknown substance was endowed with a pungent energy of life, even though it was only to be found inside the dead. There was none of it in the living: on the contrary, they had patches of death in them, gathering inside them long before they met their end. Sambikin then fell into perplexity for several years, and this perplexity had still not left him: how was it that a corpse, even if only briefly, could be a reservoir of the most sudden, thrusting life? Investigating more precisely, speculating about all this almost constantly, Sambikin came to believe that at the moment of death some kind of hidden sluice must open in the human body, and that from it there flows through the organism a special fluid which poisons the pus of death and washes away the ash of exhaustion, and which is carefully preserved all through life, right up to the moment of supreme danger. But where in the darkness, in the clefts of the human body, is this sluice that so jealously and faithfully preserves the last charge of life? Only death, when it rushes through the body, can break the seal on that reserve of concentrated life – and then, like an unsuccessful shot, this life resounds inside a person for the last time, leaving vague traces on his dead heart . . . A fresh corpse was permeated through and through with traces of this secret, now motionless substance, and every part of a dead person preserved a creative strength for those who were left to go on living. Sambikin's intention was to transform the dead into a force that would nourish the longevity and health of the living. He had understood the chastity and power of that youthful fluid that bathes a person's insides at the moment of his last breath; this fluid, incorporated into someone who was alive but wilting, would be able to render that person upright, steadfast and happy.[15]

Sartorius stood on the balcony for a long time; everything now seemed undecided and irrelevant. Unknown people were going down the street in a tram. Sounds of traffic and fragments of conversation reached his ears as if from far away; he listened to them without interest or curiosity, as though he were sick and alone. What he wanted now was to go straight home, to lie down under a blanket and warm his sudden pain, so it would leave him by morning, when it was time for him to get going again.

Behind his back, his contemporaries were delighting in the consciousness of their own success and of the future technological dream. Muldbauer was speaking about a stratum of the atmosphere, at an altitude of something between 50 and 100 kilometres, where the light, temperature and electromagnetic conditions were such that a living organism would neither tire nor die; on the contrary, it would be capable of eternal existence amid violet space. This was the "Heaven" of the ancients and the happy land of the people of the future; far beyond the expanse of stormy weather that spread out down below, there did indeed lie a blessèd country. Muldbauer was predicting the imminent conquest of the stratosphere and a subsequent penetration into these blue heights where the airy country of immortality lay; man would then become wingèd, while the earth would be inherited by the animals and would once again, and forever, be covered over by the dense forests of its ancient virginity. "And the animals know this!" Muldbauer was saying with conviction. "When I look into their eyes, they seem to be thinking: 'When will all this come to an end? When will you finally leave us? When will you leave us alone to follow our own fate?'"

Sartorius smiled bleakly; he would have liked to remain at the very bottom of the earth, or even to settle in an empty tomb and, never parting from Moscow Chestnova, live out his life there until death. But it would be a pity to leave unanswered these night stars that had been looking at him since childhood, to play no part in a universal life now filled by labour and a feeling of closeness between people; he was afraid of walking through the city mutely, his head bowed, with the concentrated and solitary thought of love, and he had no wish to grow indifferent to his desk – which was heaped with the drafts and plans of his ideas – to the iron bed he had lain on for so long, or to his desk lamp, his patient witness in the darkness and silence of working nights . . . Sartorius stroked his chest beneath his shirt and said to himself: "Go away! Leave me on my own again, vile element! I'm a straightforward engineer and a rationalist, and I reject you as woman and as love. I'd do better to worship electrons and atomic dust!" But the world, spread out before him as fire and noise, was already dying into soundlessness; it had drifted away beyond the dark threshold of his heart and left behind it only a single being – the most touching creature on earth. Could he really renounce this being in order to devote himself to the atom – to a mere particle of dust and ash?

Moscow Chestnova joined Sartorius on the balcony, and said to him with a smile, "Why are you so sad? Do you love me or not?"

She was breathing on him with the warmth of her smiling mouth and her dress was rustling. Sartorius was gripped by a vain obstinacy of malice and bravado. He answered, "No, I'm admiring another Moscow – the city."

"All right then," said Moscow, readily accepting this. "Let's go and eat. Comrade Selin is eating more than anyone. He's really stuffed himself, he looks quite red, but his eyes are always sad. You don't know why, do you?"

"No," said Sartorius quietly. "I'm sad too."

Moscow peered through the dark at his disproportionately large face; his eyes were open, and tears were running down his cheeks.

"There's no need to cry," said Moscow. "I love you too."

"You're lying," said Sartorius.

"No, it's true, it's really true!" exclaimed Moscow. "Come on, let's get away from here!"

As they walked arm in arm through their celebrating friends, Sambikin watched them through eyes that had forgotten how to blink and that had been carried away by thought to a place far distant from personal happiness. Near the exit Bozhko suddenly appeared right in front of Moscow and respectfully pronounced his patient request. Moscow was so pleased to see him that she snatched a piece of cake from the table and immediately offered it to him.

Viktor Vasilievich Bozhko was now working at the weights and measures institute and was entirely engrossed by weighing and measuring instruments. He asked Moscow to introduce him to this famous engineer, someone who might be able to invent simple and accurate scales that could be manufactured cheaply for all the collective and state farms and for the whole of Soviet commerce. Not noticing Sartorius's sadness, Bozhko immediately began to speak about the great and unnoticed problems of the national economy: the additional difficulties experienced by socialism on the collective farms, the reduced payments to collective-farmers, *kulak* policies that exploited the inaccuracy of weights, scales and balances, and the massive, if involuntary, defrauding of working-class consumers in co-operatives and distribution centres . . . None of which would occur if it were not for the dilapidated condition of the State's stock of scales and balances, the antiquated design of the scales and the shortage of metal and wood for the fabrication of new weighing machines.

"You must excuse me," said Bozhko, "I came here in spite of myself. I know I'm being tedious. People here have been talking – and I've been listening to them – about how man will soon be winged and happy. It will always be a pleasure to me to hear this, but what we need at the moment is something much less. We need our collective farmers to be able to weigh flour and grain with accuracy."

Moscow smiled at him with the gentleness of her transient self: "You're splendid, you're a true Soviet man! Sartorius, go along to their institute tomorrow and design them the cheapest and simplest of scales – and make sure they're accurate!"

Sartorius fell into thought. "That's difficult," he admitted. "It's easier to perfect a steam-engine than a pair of scales. Scales have been used for thousands of years. It would be like inventing a new kind of bucket for water. But I'll come to your institute and do what I can for you."

7

THEY REACHED THE OUTSKIRTS OF THE CITY ON ALMOST the last tram, and there was no going back. The sky above the horizon reflected a distant electrical glow onto the earth, and the faintest, poorest of lights reached as far as the fields, lying on the ears of rye like a false, early dawn. But it was still the middle of the night.

Moscow Chestnova took off her shoes and began to walk barefoot over the softness of the earth. Sartorius followed her in fear and joy; there was nothing she could do now that didn't bring trembling into his heart, and he was afraid of the anxious and dangerous life that was unfolding there. He followed after her, continually lagging behind without meaning to, thinking about her monotonously, but with such tenderness that if Moscow had squatted down to pee, Sartorius would have begun to cry.

Moscow gave him her shoes to carry. Without her noticing, he sniffed them and even touched them with his tongue; now neither Moscow Chestnova herself, nor anything about her, however dirty, could have made Sartorius feel in the least squeamish, and he could have looked at the waste products of her body with the greatest of interest, since they too had not long ago formed part of a splendid person.

"Comrade Sartorius, what are we going to do now?" asked Moscow. "It's still night, soon there'll be dew on the ground."

"I don't know," Sartorius answered morosely. "Probably I'll have to love you."

"There's a collective farm asleep in that hollow over there," said Moscow, pointing into the distance. "There'll be a smell of bread, and little children snuffling away in the barns. And cows are lying in the pasture, and a dawn mist is forming above them. How I love seeing all this and being alive!"

No cows or little children snuffling in their sleep meant anything to Sartorius now. He would even have liked the earth to become suddenly deserted, so there would be nothing to distract Moscow's attention, and she would concentrate only on him.

Towards dawn Moscow and Sartorius sat down in a land surveyor's pit; it was overgrown with tall warm weeds that had taken refuge there from the cultured fields like *kulaks* hiding away in their farmsteads.

Sartorius took Moscow by the hand. All of nature – everything that flowed through the mind as thought, that drove the heart onward and was revealed to the gaze, always in an unfamiliar and primordial guise, as overgrown grass, as life's unique days, as the vast sky, as people's nearby faces – all of this nature was for Sartorius now enclosed in one body, ending at the hem of her dress, at the ends of her bare feet.

Sartorius's youth had been spent in the study of physics and mechanics; he had laboured over the computation of infinity as a body, trying to work out an economical explanation for its functioning. He had wanted to discover, in the very flow of human consciousness, a thought that was in resonance with nature and so – even if only by chance, by living chance – reflected the whole of nature's truth; and he had hoped to secure this thought for ever through some calculable formula. But now he was not conscious of any thought at all because his heart had risen up into his head and was beating there above his eyes. Sartorius stroked Moscow's hand, which was firm and full, like a reservoir of sparing, tightly compressed feeling.

"Tell me, Semyon, what is it you want from me?" Moscow asked meekly, ready for kindness.

"I want to marry you," said Sartorius. "I don't know what else to want."

Moscow fell into thought, and she ate a blade of long grass with her young, avid mouth.

"Yes, it's true – there's nothing else to want when you're in love. But people say that's being stupid."

"Let people say what they like," said Sartorius gloomily. "All they do is talk – probably they've never loved . . . What can I do if I ache for you like this?"

"Hug me then, and I'll hug you."

Sartorius hugged her.

"Well, is your ache any better now?"

"No, it's just the same," Sartorius answered.

"Then we'll have to get married," Moscow agreed.

When an innocent, everyday morning lit up the local collective farms and the outskirts of the huge city, Moscow and Sartorius were still in the land surveyor's pit. Having known the whole of Moscow in full – all the warmth, devotion and happiness of her body – Sartorius found with surprise and horror that his love had not exhausted itself but had increased, and that essentially he had achieved nothing, and still remained as unhappy as he had been before. Which meant that this was not the way to attain another person and truly share life with them. How then should one exist? Sartorius had no idea.

Moscow Chestnova was lying on her back. At first the sky above her was watery; then it became blue and stone-like; then it turned into something golden and sparkling, as if blooming with colours – the sun had risen behind the Urals, and it was drawing closer.

Moscow clambered out of the pit, straightened her dress, put her shoes on and set off towards the city alone. She had told Sartorius that she would be his wife later; for the time being he should work at the Institute for Weights and Measures, together with Bozhko – she would find him there when the time was right.

Helpless and worthless, Sartorius came out after her. He stood alone in the dawn, in the emptiness of the unripe fields, dirty and sad, like a surviving warrior on a silent battle-ground.

"But why are you going, Moscow? I love you more than ever!"

Moscow turned to face him: "I'm not leaving you, Semyon. I've already said I'll be back. I love you too."

"Then why are you going? Come back here again."

Moscow was standing in bewilderment about ten yards away.

"I'm sorry, Semyon."

"What are you sorry about?"

"I'm sorry about something . . . No matter how long I live, life never turns out like I want it to."

Moscow frowned, standing sullenly on the edge of the tall rye. The sun was shining on the silk of her dress, and the last drops of morning moisture, gathered from the tall grass, were drying on her hair. A light breeze was blowing from the basin of the Moscow River, and the swollen ears of rye were murmuring vaguely; like a thought or a smile, the light of the sun had filled the whole area. Only Moscow did not share this cheerfulness, and her beautiful dress and her body, both made from this same glittering nature, seemed out of keeping with her sad face. Sartorius led Moscow back to their grassy hiding-place, unable to understand why they both felt so bleak.

"Leave me alone!" said Moscow, suddenly moving away from Sartorius. "I've done everything, I've flown in the air and I've had husbands – you're not the first, my sad, dear man!"

Moscow turned away and lay face down on the ground. The sight of her large, incomprehensible body, warmed beneath the skin by hidden blood, compelled Sartorius to embrace Moscow and once again, silently and hurriedly, expend with her a part of his life: what else could he do – even though this was something poor and unnecessary and, far from resolving love, merely left a man exhausted? But before Sartorius's embraces were over, Moscow turned her face to him and smiled mockingly – in some way she was deceiving the man she loved.

Sartorius got to his feet, just as if nothing had happened. He was perplexed: the weeping force of feeling that pulled him towards her had not received any consolation – his heart still ached for Moscow, as vainly as though she had died or were beyond his reach.

"You probably don't love me!" he said, trying to guess her secret.

"No, I do, I really like you," Moscow tried to convince him. "I'm not finding this easy either."

Somewhere in the distance collective-farm carts were already moving over the earth; it was time to go to work in the city, for the two of them to go their separate ways and leave one another.

Moscow was sitting sullenly on the grass. As for Sartorius, he was now reconciled to his love for her; it would be enough to live with Moscow in marriage, to admire her, perhaps to have children – and then the pain of his feelings would fade, his heart would wear itself out, quietening down for ever so his mind could engage in calm and fertile mental activity.

"When I was a child," Moscow told him, "I saw a man running down the street at night with fire on the end of a stick, with a torch. He was running to the people in the prison, he wanted to burn it down."

"There was a lot of that sort of thing," said Sartorius.

"I feel sorry for him all the time. He was killed."

"What's so special about that?" asked Sartorius in surprise. "A lot of dead people are lying in the earth; there'll probably never be a heart that can remember all the dead at once, and can weep for them. What would be the use of a heart like that?"

Moscow fell silent for a while; she was looking at everything with lifeless eyes, as though she were ill.

"You know what, Semyon? It would be better if you stopped loving me. I've loved a lot of men already, but for you I'm the first! You're a virgin, while I'm a woman!"

Sartorius said nothing. Moscow put one arm round him.

"Really, Semyon – stop loving me! Do you know how much thinking and feeling I've done? It's terrible. And nothing's come of it."

"What hasn't come of it?" asked Sartorius.

"Life hasn't come of it. I'm afraid it never will, and I'm in a hurry now . . . I saw a woman once, she was pressing her face to the wall and she was crying. She was crying from grief – she was 34 years old, and grieving so badly for the time of her past that I thought she had lost 100 roubles or more."

"No, Moscow, I love you," said Sartorius gloomily. "I'll feel good living with you."

"But I won't feel good living with you," said Moscow. "And you won't feel good living with me – so why lie and pretend that you will? I've wanted so many times to share my life with someone, and that's what I still do want – I've never been sparing with my life and I never will be! What good is my life to me without people, without the whole of the USSR? If I'm a Komsomol member, it's not because I was poor when I was a little girl . . ."

Moscow was speaking with bitterness, with seriousness, like an experienced old woman who has lived her life all the way through. She had withered there and then – because of the weakness of her heart, which was now clenched inside her breast as if in some unknown darkness.

"To make you believe me, I'm going to kiss you!"

Moscow kissed Sartorius, who had gone mute with sorrow. He could do nothing but watch with terror the sudden aging of her evident beauty, yet this made his love for her all the stronger.

"I've just worked it out – why it is that people's lives together are so bad. It's because it's impossible to unite through love. I've tried so many times, but nothing ever comes of it – nothing but a little pleasure. You were with me just now – and what did you feel? Something astonishing? Something wonderful? Or nothing much?"

"Nothing much," admitted Sartorius.

"My skin always feels cold afterwards," said Moscow. "Love cannot be communism. I've thought and thought and I've realized that it just can't. One probably should love – and I will love. But it's like eating food – it's just a necessity, it's not what matters in life."

Sartorius was upset that his love, which he had saved up all his life, should meekly perish the very first time. But he understood Moscow's painful thought: that the very best of feelings lies in understanding another human being, sharing the burdens and happiness of a second, unknown life, and that the love which comes with embraces brings only a child-like, blissful joy, and does nothing to solve the problem of drawing people into the mystery of a shared existence.

"What can you and I do now?" asked Sartorius.

"We'll be around a long time yet," Moscow smiled. "Wait for me, and work with Bozhko at the weights and scales factory – I'll come to you again. But now I'm going away."

"Where to? Sit with me a bit longer," said Sartorius.

"No, I've got to go," said Moscow, and got up from the ground.

The sun had already grown smaller in the sky and was giving off a concentrated incandescence. Locomotives were humming on the spur lines of a nearby construction site; small aeroplanes were flying through the sky on training flights; logs were being dragged by five-ton trucks, grinding the soil to dust – heat and work had been spreading across the world since dawn.

Moscow said goodbye to Sartorius, taking his head in her hands. She was happy again, she wanted to go away into the incalculable life that had long tormented her heart with a premonition of unknown pleasure – into the darkness of people and crowds, so as to live out with them the mystery of her existence.

She went away content, keeping her satisfaction in check; she felt like throwing her dress off and running straight ahead, as though she were on the shore of some southern sea.

Sartorius was left on his own. He wanted Moscow to return to him, and for them to become husband and wife trustingly and for ever. Sartorius could feel his body being penetrated by sorrow and by indifference to the interests of life – confused and tormenting forces had arisen within him and eclipsed all of his mind, all healthy action towards a more distant aim. But Sartorius was willing to exhaust in Moscow's embraces everything tender, strange and human that had appeared in him – anything to make his sense of himself less difficult, to be able to give himself once again to the clear movement of thought, and to long, daily labour in the ranks of his patient comrades. He wanted to protect himself against all present or future convulsions in his life by means of a simple, beloved wife, and so he decided to wait for Moscow's return.

8

THE INSTITUTE WAS ON THE EVE OF BEING LIQUIDATED. Only later did Sartorius understand that what is destined for liquidation can sometimes prove to be not only the most durable of all, but even to be doomed to eternal existence. The institute was housed in the Old Merchants' Arcade, in a gallery that had once been a storage place for goods vulnerable to damp. A staircase went down from the institute into the stone arcade that had formerly surrounded the whole of the merchants' courtyard. On the main door was a metal plate: THE MEASURE OF LABOUR: THE INSTITUTE FOR SCALES, WEIGHTS AND MEASURES.[16]

The management office of this poor, half-forgotten branch of heavy industry was a single large and gloomy room with a low ceiling like that of an underground vault; where it met the walls, the ceiling came down so low that the employees sitting there almost touched it with their heads. There were a number of desks in the room, with one or two people at each of them, either writing or counting on abacuses. There were only around 30 employees, and certainly not more than 40, but with the noise of their work, with their movements, questions and exclamations, they created the impression that this was a huge institution of the highest importance.

Sartorius was immediately taken on as engineer responsible for the design of new scales, and he sat down at a table opposite Viktor Vasilievich Bozhko.

And the days of his new life began. In the course of a few nights Sartorius finished his last project from his previous workplace, the Institute for Experimental Mechanical Engineering, and began to focus his attention on the most ancient machine in the world – the balance. Nothing has changed so little in the course of the last 5,000 years of history as the balance. At the time of the Cyclopes, in ancient Greece and Carthage, in mighty Persia that was felled by the blows of Alexander of Macedon – everywhere, at all times and in all spaces, the most universal and indispensable machine has been the balance. Balances are as old as weapons, and it may be that they are one and the same – what is a balance but a sword from the battle, laid across the crest of a rock, so that the victors can divide up the booty with justice?

Bozhko, who was unable to work unless he felt love, in both mind and heart, for the object of the task entrusted to him, expounded at length to Sartorius on the decisive importance of the balance in the life of humanity. "The late Dmitry Ivanovich Mendeleev himself," he said, "loved scales more than anything in the world. Not even his own periodic table of the elements meant more to him. And that's hardly surprising. After all, the whole thing is based on the balance. Atomic weight – that's all there is to it!"

Bozhko also knew why a weighing apparatus is the most paltry and insignificant of objects. People pay close attention only to what lies on the balance; they see the sausage or the bread, but don't notice what's beneath them. Beneath the sausage or bread, however, is the balance, the instrument of honour and justice, a simple pauper of a machine that counts and takes care of the sacred bounty of socialism, measuring out the food of both factory workers and collective-farm workers according to their creative labour and the principles of accounting.

With diligence, with a miserly concern for the crumbs of bread that are lost as a result of the inaccuracy of balances,

Sartorius immersed himself in his work. Unknown to anyone, two feelings had met and combined together inside him – love for Moscow Chestnova and anticipation of socialism. His vague imagination held out a picture of summer: tall rye, the voices of millions of people who, for the first time, were organizing themselves on earth without being dragged down by poverty and sadness, and Moscow Chestnova, coming towards him from far away to be his wife. She had gone the rounds of life; together with countless others she had lived life through and had left the years of emotions and suffering behind her, in the darkness of her past youth; she was returning the same as she always had been, only barefoot, in a poor dress, with hands that had grown bigger from work, and yet she was clearer and merrier than before; she had found contentment for her wandering heart.

Her wandering heart! For a long time the human heart quakes in foreboding, gripped by bones and by the misery of everyday life – and at last it rushes forward, losing its warmth on roads that are cold and chilly.

Bent over his desk in the institute, Sartorius worked as fast as he could on improving the construction of the balance. The director informed him of the danger of weight riots on the collective farms, like the salt riots of old, since an inadequate balance means either a short measure of bread in payment for work, or else – if too much bread is issued – a defrauding of the State. Moreover, the platforms of freight scales – if the scales were inaccurate – could become arenas of *kulak* politics and class warfare. Another problem fraught with potential danger was constituted by the weights themselves. In many weighing stations, instead of using officially stamped weights, they had been placing all kinds of mad nonsense on the balances: bricks, pig-iron, and there had even been cases of pregnant women being sat on a balance and being paid, as if for a day's work, for hiring out their torsos. All this must lead inevitably to the loss of billions of kilos of grain.

Grieving for Moscow, afraid of life alone in his room, Sartorius would sometimes stay in the institute all night long. At ten o'clock in the evening the night watchman would take a preliminary nap on a chair by the entrance; a little later he would retire to the director's office, settling down in the soft armchair behind the plywood partition. Time passed on the big official clock; the empty desks made Sartorius long for the other employees; sometimes mice would appear and look at him with meek eyes.

He sat on his own, working at the same problem that Archimedes had thought about in his day, and that Mendeleev had pondered more recently. He could find no solution: the balance was all right as it was – but there was a need for something different, something better, something that would require less metal to manufacture. Sartorius covered sheet after sheet of paper with calculations of prisms, levers, deformation tensions, costs of materials and other data. Suddenly, of their own accord, tears would come out of his eyes and flow down his face, and Sartorius would feel astonished at this phenomenon: something was living in the depths of his body, some kind of separate animal, and it was weeping silently, and taking no interest in the manufacture of balances. After midnight, when the smell of distant plants and fresh open spaces wafted over the entire city and came in through the open ventilation pane, Sartorius would lose his precision of thought and lay his head down on the desk. Once, close beside him, Moscow Chestnova had given off the same smell of nature and kindness. He no longer felt jealous:

let her eat good food and plenty of it, let her not fall ill, let her enjoy life, let her love people she met and then go to sleep somewhere warm, with no memory of any unhappiness.

Once or twice a night the telephone would suddenly ring, and Sartorius would hurriedly listen to the receiver, but nobody was calling him; it was a wrong number and the other person would apologize and disappear for ever into silence. Not one of his many friends knew what had happened to Sartorius: he had abandoned the high road of technology and would not be returning to it for a long time to come, forgetting his fame as a mechanical engineer, which could have become world-wide.

One day Sambikin called on Sartorius at home. The surgeon told Sartorius that the spinal cord of a human being was endowed with a certain capacity for rational thought, that it was not only the mind in the head that could think; he had recently checked this hypothesis on a child on whom he was performing a second trepanning – he had had to remove [. . .][17]

"But where does all this get us?" Sartorius asked without enthusiasm.

"It's the fundamental secret of life, more particularly it's the secret of the human being as a whole," Sambikin said thoughtfully. "In the past it was held that the spinal cord concerned itself only with the heart and with purely organic functions, and that the brain was the higher coordinating centre. That's not true: the spinal cord can indeed think – while the brain, for its part, is involved in the simplest, most instinctive processes."

Sambikin's discovery had made him happy. He still believed it was possible to ascend in one bound to a mountain peak from which times and spaces would become visible to the ordinary grey gaze of man. Sartorius smiled a little at Sambikin's naiveté: nature was too difficult, by his own reckoning, for such instant victories, and could not be confined within a single law.

"Well, go on!" said Sartorius.

Sambikin's insides began to gurgle from the noise of his higher feelings.

"Well . . . This needs to be confirmed experimentally a thousand times. But it could well be that the secret of life lies in man's dual consciousness. We always think two thoughts at once, we can't think just one! We have two organs for one task! They think about the same subject, they think towards one another . . . Do you realize this could be the foundation of a truly scientific, dialectical psychology such as the world has never seen before? The fact that a human being is capable of thinking doubly about every subject is what has made him the finest animal on earth."

"What about the other animals?" asked Sartorius. "They've got heads and spines too."

"True. But there's a difference – a trifling difference that has decided world history. It was necessary to get used to coordinating two thoughts, to uniting in a single impulse one thought that rises from out of the earth itself, from deep in the bones, and another that descends from the heights of the skull. It was necessary that these thoughts should always meet together, that their waves should coincide and resonate. Animals are the same: they too have two thoughts in response to each impression, but their two thoughts wander off in different directions and don't join together to make a single impact. That's the secret of human evolution, that's why man has left all the other animals behind! What enabled him to carry it off was something almost trifling: he was able to train two feelings, two obscure currents, to meet and measure their strength against each other . . . And when they meet, they are transformed into human thought. It goes without saying that none of this is perceptible . . . Animals can experience these states too, but only occasionally and by chance. But man has been nurtured by this same chance, he has become a dual being. And sometimes, in illness, in unhappiness, in love, in a terrible dream, at any moment, in fact, that's remote from the normal, we clearly sense that there are two of us – that I am one person but there's someone else inside me as well. This someone, this mysterious 'he', often mutters and sometimes weeps, he wants to get out from inside you and go a long way away, he gets bored, he feels frightened . . . We can see there are two of us and that we've had enough of one another. We imagine the lightness, the freedom, the senseless paradise of the animals when our consciousness was not dual but single. Only a hair's breadth separates us from an animal when we lose the duality of our consciousness, and very often we live in archaic times without understanding what that means . . . But then our two consciousnesses couple together again, we once again become human beings in the embrace of our 'two-edged' thought, and nature, organized according to the principle of an impoverished singleness, grits her teeth and curls herself up to escape from the activity of these terrible dual structures which she never engendered, which came into being inside their own selves . . . I find it so terrifying now to be on my own! These two passions eternally copulating and warming my head . . ."

Sambikin, who had obviously not eaten or slept for a long time, ran out of strength and sat down in despair.

Sartorius gave him some tinned food and some vodka. Gradually the two of them grew quiet from tiredness and lay down to sleep without undressing, leaving the electricity burning, while their hearts and minds continued to stir mutely inside them, hurrying to sort out both ordinary feelings and world-historical tasks in the time allotted.

Midnight had long ago chimed from the Spassky Tower, and the music of the Internationale[18] had fallen silent; soon it would be dawn and, in anticipation of this, the tenderest birds, those who stayed the shortest time, began to rustle in the bushes and gardens; then they rose up and flew away, leaving a country where summer had already begun to cool.

When day began and the street-lamps turned yellow, the tall Sambikin and the short Sartorius were still asleep on the one sofa, breathing noisily as if they had hollow bodies. Though it was inhibited by sleep, their yearning for a definitive structuring of the world still gnawed at their consciences, and from time to time they muttered words, to drive out anxiety. Where was Moscow Chestnova? Where was she sleeping now? What summer of life was she seeking at the beginning of autumn, leaving her friends to wait in expectation?

Near the end of his sleep, Sartorius smiled. Meek by nature, he felt that he had died and been buried in the earth, in its deep warmth, while up above, on the daytime surface of the grave, only Moscow Chestnova was left to weep for him. There was no one else; he had died nameless, like a man who had truly carried out all his tasks. The Republic was now sated with balances, overstocked with them, and the entire arithmetical computation of future historical time had been completed, so that life would be made secure and would never be confronted by despair.

He woke up satisfied, resolved to construct and bring to perfection a complete technological apparatus that would automatically pump the basic vital force of food out of nature and into the human body. But, early though it was, his eyes had turned pale from the memory of Moscow; moved by fear of suffering, he woke Sambikin.

"Sambikin!" he asked. "You're a doctor, you know the whole reason for life . . . Why does life go on for so long, and how can it be comforted or made happy for ever?"

"Sartorius!" Sambikin answered jokingly. "You're a mechanic, you know what a vacuum is . . ."

"Well, yes. An emptiness into which something is sucked."

"An emptiness," said Sambikin. "Come with me, I'll show you the reason for all life."

They went out and set off on a tram. Sartorius looked out of the window and met about 100,000 people, but nowhere did he notice the face of Moscow Chestnova. She might even have died – after all, time moves on and chance events happen.

They arrived at the surgical clinic of the Institute for Experimental Medicine. "I'm dissecting four corpses today," Sambikin announced. "There are three of us here working on one problem: how to obtain a certain mysterious substance, traces of which are present in every fresh corpse. This substance has the most powerful vivifying power for the living, tired organism. What this substance is – we don't know! But we're trying to find out."

Sambikin prepared himself as usual, and then led Sartorius to the dissecting room. This was a large, cold room where four dead people were lying in boxes that had ice between their double walls.

Sambikin's two assistants took the body of a young woman from one of these boxes and laid it out before the surgeon on an inclined table like an enlarged music stand. The woman lay there with clear, open eyes; the substance of these eyes was so lacking in feeling that it could go on shining even after life, so long as it did not begin to decompose. Sartorius felt ill. He decided to run out of the clinic and back to his institute; then he could go to the trade-union committee and ask for comradely protection against the terror of his yearning heart.

"All right," said Sambikin, now ready for work. He then explained to Sartorius: "At the moment of death a last sluice opens in the human body, one that we know little about. Behind that sluice, in some dark cleft of the organism, a last charge of life is jealously and faithfully preserved. Nothing but death can open up that spring, that reservoir – it remains tightly sealed until the very end. But I shall find that cistern of immortality."

"That's good," uttered Sartorius.

Sambikin cut the left breast off the woman, then removed all the bars of the ribcage and, with the utmost caution, made his way to the heart. Together with his assistants he removed the heart and carefully, using his instruments, put it in a glass cylinder for further investigation; this cylinder was then taken off to the laboratory.

"This heart too bears traces of the unknown secretion I was telling you about," Sambikin told his friend. "Death, when it rushes through the body, breaks the seal on that reserve of concentrated life – and then, like an unsuccessful shot, life resounds inside a person for the last time, leaving faint traces on his dead heart. But that substance, because of its energy, is something extremely precious. It's very strange – what's most vital of all appears at the moment of the last breath. Nature guards her procedures carefully!"

Then Sambikin began to roll the dead girl from side to side, as if to demonstrate to Sartorius her plumpness and chastity.

"She's good-looking," the surgeon said vaguely; the thought went through his mind that he could marry this dead woman – who was more beautiful, faithful and lonely than many of the living – and he carefully bandaged up her ruined chest. "And now," he went on, "we shall see the general reason for life."

Sambikin opened up the fatty envelope of the stomach, and then guided his knife down the intestine, revealing its contents: inside lay an unbroken column of food that had not yet been assimilated, but soon this food came to an end and the intestine was empty. Sambikin went slowly down the section of emptiness and reached the beginning of the excrement, where he came to a stop.

"You see!" said Sambikin, opening more widely the slit down the empty section between the food and the excrement. "This emptiness in the intestines sucks all humanity into itself and is the moving force of world history. This is the soul – have a sniff!"[19]

Sartorius had a sniff. "It's nothing special!" he said. "We shall fill that emptiness. Then some other thing will become the soul."

"But what?" said Sambikin, smiling.

"I don't know," said Sartorius, feeling a pitiful humiliation. "First people must be fed properly, so they won't be drawn into the emptiness of the intestines . . ."

"If you don't have a soul, it's impossible either to feed anyone or to have enough to eat yourself,"[20] Sambikin replied bleakly. "Nothing's possible."

Sartorius bent down over the entrails of the corpse, over the place in the intestines where man's empty soul lay. He touched the remnants of excrement and food with his fingers, carefully studied the cramped, impoverished layout of the whole body, and said, "This really is the very best, ordinary soul. There's no other soul anywhere."

The engineer turned towards the exit from the department of corpses. He stooped down and left, sensing behind him the smile of Sambikin. He was distressed by the sorrow and poverty of life, distressed that life was so helpless that it needed almost constant illusions in order to distract itself from a consciousness of its true situation. Even Sambikin was seeking illusions in his ideas and discoveries – he too was carried away by the complexity and great essence the world possessed in his imagination. But Sartorius could see that the world consisted primarily of destitute matter, which it was almost impossible to love but essential to understand.

9

MOSCOW CHESTNOVA DID NOT KNOW WHAT TO DO WITH herself after deciding not to return to her room and not to love Sartorius any more. For long hours she travelled about the city, walking or taking buses and trams; no one approached her or asked her anything. The whole of life rushed by around her, so petty and rubbishy that it made Moscow feel people were united by nothing at all and that the space between them was occupied by bewilderment.

Towards evening she set off towards the housing co-operative where the reservist lived. The fiddler was tuning his fiddle by the entrance to the house management office; from the other side of the fence, where the medical institute was being constructed, came the whine of a circular saw; and the inhabitants of the housing co-operative were gathering in the corridor for their usual conversations.

Reservist Komyagin was lying on an iron bed in his little room. He had been looking vainly inside himself for some thought or other, for some feeling or state of mind, but he had realized there was nothing there. He would try to think about something, yet would lose interest in the object of his reflection before he had even started, and so would abandon the desire to think. But if some enigma did happen to appear in his consciousness, he would be unable to resolve it, and it would ache away in his brain until he physically annihilated it by means of, for instance, intensified life with women and long sleep. He would then wake up empty and calm, with no recollection of his inner distress. Sometimes suffering or irritation would spring up inside him, like weeds on waste ground, but Komyagin soon transformed them into empty indifference with the help of these measures.

But in recent years he had grown tired of struggling against what was human in him, and sometimes he cried in the darkness, covering his face with a blanket that had not been washed since the day of its manufacture.

Long ago, however, there had been a time when Komyagin led an unusual life. The walls of his room were still hung with unfinished oil paintings depicting Rome, landscapes, various peasant huts, and rye growing above hollows. Komyagin had begun work on them but had not managed to finish even one picture, though at least ten years of time had gone by; and so the little huts had remained in a state of ruin, with no roofs, the rye had never come into ear, and Rome looked like some provincial town. Somewhere under the bed, among the outlived objects, lay an exercise book of poems he had begun in his youth and a whole diary, also without any conclusion, broken off in the middle of a word as if someone had hit Komyagin and he had dropped his pen for ever. About three years ago Komyagin had wanted to make a list of his clothes and other belongings, but this too he had failed to complete, managing to write down only four items: himself, the bed, the blanket and the chair. Everything else was waiting to be taken stock of in some future, better time.

Recently Komyagin had been looking everywhere for a button and had found the exercise book with the poems he had begun. They were about village life. He had read the beginning of one poem:

> In that night, O in that night, the sleep of field and
>   farm was light;
> Paths called out to them in silence, stretching out
>   towards a star,
> And the steppe in languor breathing, bare of body, quiet
>   of heart,
> Seemed to stand in fear upon a trembling bridge that
>   floated far.

The poem had no ending. The one and only chair could not stand on its legs and was in need of urgent repair – Komyagin had once even acquired two nails for this purpose, but had not yet got down to work.

Sometimes Komyagin would think to himself: "In a month or two I shall begin a new life – I'll finish the paintings and poems; I'll thoroughly rethink my world outlook; I'll get my documents in order; I'll find myself a solid job and become an exemplary shock-worker; I'll fall in love with some woman and she can be a wife and a friend to me." It was his hope that in a month or two something special would happen to time, that it would stop for a moment and take him up into its movement, but the years passed by his window without any pause or fortunate event. And so he would get up from his bed and go out, as a member of the volunteer militia, to exact fines from the general public at the sites where it most tended to accumulate.

Now it was August of one of these passing years. Evening was drawing in, spreading across the sky a long sad sound that receded into the distance and caused regret and a brooding melancholy to penetrate every heart that was open. Moscow Chestnova knocked on Komyagin's door. Without getting up from the bed, he threw the hook off the door with his left hand

and invited his guest to come in. She went inside, strange and familiar, in her expensive dress, and she looked round as though this were the room she was used to living in. The reservist decided to surrender immediately: his papers were not in order and he had no excuse. But Moscow merely asked him how his life was going, and wasn't it sad to be so alone and useless?

"I'm all right," said Komyagin. "After all, I'm not living – life's just something I'm caught up in. It's a pointless business – but somehow or other I got dragged into it."

"Why is it pointless?" asked Moscow.

"I just can't be bothered," said Komyagin. "You keep having to puff yourself up – you have to think, speak, go somewhere or other, do this and that. But I can't be bothered with anything. I keep forgetting that I'm alive – and when I remember, it scares me."

Moscow decided to stay a bit longer, astonished at the way of life of this man who had been begun so long ago and yet was still unfinished. Komyagin warmed up some *kasha* to give her for supper, and then showed her his favourite painting from a time Moscow had never known. It had been lying among the junk tucked away under the bed; the painting was not completely finished, but the message had been expressed with clarity.

"If the State didn't object, I should live like that too," said Komyagin.

The picture portrayed a peasant or merchant – someone who was quite well off, but dirty and barefoot. He was standing on a rickety wooden porch and, from this high spot, was peeing downwards. His shirt was billowing in the wind, there were bits of dirt and straw in his tatty little beard, and he was looking indifferently into a desolate world where a pale sun was either rising or setting. Behind the man was a large forlorn-looking house; inside it, most likely, were stores of food – pies and pots of jam – and a wooden bed, made ready for an almost eternal sleep. An aging peasant woman was sitting on an enclosed verandah – all you could see was her head – and looking, with a foolish expression, into an empty space in the yard. The man had just woken from sleep, and now he had gone out to relieve himself and check whether anything in particular had chanced to happen – but everything remained the same, the wind was blowing from across ragged, unfriendly fields, and in a moment the man would return to his rest, to sleep and dream no dreams, so as to get through life quickly and without consciousness.

After a while Komyagin's divorced wife came round, an old, worn-down woman who had been exhausted for many years. She very seldom visited Komyagin, and evidently still touched his feelings through some memory of their former affection. Komyagin put out some food for his guests, but the former wife just drank up her tea in silence and got ready to leave, so as not to prevent her husband from being alone with this plump new tart of his – as she described Moscow to herself. In her eyes everyone else was plump, and she herself was the only woman no one was interested in. Komyagin, however, took Moscow out into the corridor and asked her to go outside for a little walk and then come back again if she needed to.

"I get all weak if I don't have a bit of time with a woman," Komyagin confessed. "I don't know what to do with myself, nothing interests me. And forgive me – but we're never really going to know each other."

"Yes, we are!" said Moscow, embarrassed by Komyagin's grief. "But go on now, go back to her."

Komyagin, however, stood in the corridor with her for a little longer.

"Don't take offence . . ."

"I'm not taking offence," Moscow answered. "I quite like you."

In spite of this, Komyagin began to feel upset and bowed his head.

"She used to be my wife, you see. She didn't smell good. She bore my children – and the children died. We used to go to bed without washing. She became like a brother to me, now she's growing thin and ugly. Our love has changed into something better – into shared poverty, into kinship and sorrow in one another's arms."

"I understand," Moscow said quietly. "You're like some foul little reptile, living in its little hole in the earth. I used to watch them when I was a child. I used to lie face down in a field."

"You're quite right," Komyagin agreed readily. "I'm a nothing."

Moscow frowned, thinking: "Why, why does he exist in the world? It only takes one person like him to make everyone else seem like scum – and then we beat them to death with whatever we can lay our hands on!"

"One day I'll come to you and be your wife," she said.

"I shall wait for you," Komyagin answered.

But Moscow, still an uncertain and fickle being, quickly thought better of this. "No," she said, "don't wait for me! I shall never come inside this house again – you're a miserable corpse!"

Suddenly she felt irritated and wretched, and she leaned her head against the wall. For reasons of economy, the light went out in the corridor. Komyagin went back into his room, and for a long time, through the makeshift wall, there came the sounds of worn-out love and the breathing of human exhaustion. Moscow Chestnova pressed her chest against the cold sewer-pipe that came down from the floor above; shame and fear had made her go quite still, while her heart was beating more wildly than

Komyagin's on the other side of the partition. But when she had done what he was now doing, she had not known that a third person feels just as sad, and without knowing why.

No, this was not the high road that led into the distance; the road of life did not pass through the poverty of love, or through the intestines, or through the zealous attempts of a Sartorius to comprehend precise trifles.

She went outside. It was already night. Huge clouds, lit only by their own weak light, were lying close to the surface of the city roofs and being carried away into the dark of the fields, towards the mown spaces of an empty, frenzied earth.

Moscow walked towards the centre of the city, looking into every brightly lit window she passed and stopping for a while outside several of them. Inside, people were drinking tea with their families or with guests; charming young women were playing the piano; operas and dances sounded from the loudspeakers of wirelesses; young men were arguing about matters to do with the Arctic and the stratosphere; mothers were bathing their children, and two or three counter-revolutionaries were whispering together, with a primus stove on a chair near the door, the wick turned up so the neighbours wouldn't hear them. Moscow was so interested by all that was happening in the world that she stood on tiptoe on the ledges above the buildings' foundations and gazed into people's rooms until passers-by began to laugh at her.

She went on looking for several hours, seeing joy or contentment almost everywhere yet feeling sadder and sadder herself. Everyone was occupied solely by mutual egotism with their friends, by their favourite ideas, by the warmth of their new rooms and the comfortable feeling of their own satisfaction. Moscow did not know what to attach herself to, whom to go and see, in order to live happily and normally. There was no joy for her in houses, she found no peace in the warmth of stoves or the light of table-lamps. She loved the fire that came from logs in stoves, and she loved electricity, but she loved them as though she herself were not a human being but that very same fire or electricity, the excitation of a force that brings about peace and happiness on earth.

Moscow had been feeling hungry for some time, and so she went into an all-night restaurant. She had no money at all, but she sat down and ordered a meal. The band kept on playing some insane European music that was imbued with centrifugal forces; after dancing to this music you felt like curling your body up for warmth and lying down for a long time in a narrow, secluded coffin. Paying no attention to this, Moscow joined in the dancing in the middle of the hall; almost every man present asked her to dance, seeing in her something he had lost in himself. Soon some of them were crying, burying their faces in Moscow's dress, because they had drunk too much wine, while others immediately began baring their souls to her with precision of detail. The spherical hall of the restaurant, deafened by the music and the howls of people, and filled by the torment-ing smoke of cigarettes and the gas of squeezed passions, seemed to revolve; every voice in it sounded twice, and suffering kept on being repeated. It was impossible here for anyone to break free from the ordinary – from the round ball of his head, where his thoughts rolled on along tracks laid down long ago, from the bag of the heart, where old feelings thrashed about as if they had been netted, accepting nothing new and letting go of nothing to which they were accustomed – and brief oblivion in music, or in love for a woman one had happened upon, ended either in irritation or in tears of despair. The later time got and the more the merriment thickened, the quicker the restaurant's spherical hall began to revolve; forgetting where the door was, many of the guests span round in terror on the spot, somewhere in the middle of the hall, supposing they were dancing. A middle-aged man, who had stayed silent for a long time and who had a dark light in his eyes, was treating Moscow to food with sadistic pleasure, as though what he was putting inside her were not some sweet dish, but his own kind heart. But Moscow remembered other evenings, spent with her peers; what she had seen then, beyond the open summer windows, was an ordinary field, leading into the flat expanse of infinity, and there had been no such spherical thought revolving in the chests of her comrades, eternally repeating itself until it reached its own despair – instead there had been the arrow of action and hope, tensed for irrevocable movement into the distance, into space that was straight and severe.

Night was yielding to morning. Somewhere Komyagin was sleeping with the thin woman, somewhere Sartorius was working away at the resolution of all possible problems, while the band played variations on the same old theme, as if rolling it around the inner surface of a hollow ball from which there was no way out. Moscow's partner was muttering an age-old thought about his love and sadness, and about loneliness, as he pressed his lips to the pure skin close to Moscow's elbow. Moscow said nothing. After drinking a little wine for the sake of a pause, her new acquaintance went back to telling her of his affection, and of possible happiness if only Moscow would respond with the same love.

"Your wheels are spinning round and round, but you're not moving," Moscow answered. "If you love me, then stop."

Moscow's companion did not agree. "We are born and we die on the breast of woman," he said with a slight smile. "That's what's decreed by the plot of our fate, by the whole circle of happiness."

"Well, you just keep your life on a straight line then, without any plots or circles," said Moscow. She brushed her index finger across her breasts. "Look! You'd find it difficult dying on me. I'm not soft."

A powerful, kind light appeared in the darkness of the eyes of this sudden comrade of Moscow's. He stared at her two breasts and said: "You're right, my dear. You're still very hard, yes, I can see no one's been kneading you to death. Even your nipples look straight ahead like the tips of two metal-punches. How very strange – it hurts even to look at them!"

He turned his head away in *toskà*; it was clear that his love for Moscow was growing stronger with every new thing he noticed about her, even the colour of her stockings. This was how Sartorius had loved her, and probably Sambikin too. She looked at her companion with indifference; she had no wish to meet, in a new face, someone she had already left behind. If the man sitting in front of her were another Sartorius, then she would do better to return to the first Sartorius and never leave him again.

Just before dawn the band began to play their most energetic fox-trot, one that acted even on the digestion. Moscow got up to dance with her new friend, and they danced almost alone in the middle of a hall that had been devastated by long merriment as if by some cataclysm. Many of those present were already dozing; others, surfeited with food and imaginary passions, looked on with the eyes of the dead.

The music revolved fast, like a feeling of melancholy in a round, bony head from which there is no way out. But the hidden energy of the melody was so great that it promised in time to wear a hole through the stagnant bones of loneliness or to escape through the eyes, if only as tears. Moscow knew very well that what she was doing with her arms and legs was nonsense, but there were many things she liked even though they were useless.

Beyond the window of the restaurant's spherical hall, dawn was breaking. A tree grew outside; it could be seen in the first light. Its branches grew straight up or straight out to the side, without curling or turning back on themselves, and the tree ended abruptly, all at once, where it lacked the strength or resources to go any higher. Moscow looked at it and said to herself: "Just like me! Good! Now I'll leave here for ever!"

She said goodbye to her cavalier, but he at once began grieving for her.

"Where are you going? There's no hurry. Let's go somewhere else. Just wait a moment while I pay!"

Moscow said nothing. The man carried on, "Let's go out into the fields – in front of us there'll be nothing at all, only some wind or other blowing from the dark! And it's always good out in the dark."

He smiled a strained smile, trying to hide his distress as he counted the last seconds before they parted.

"I'm afraid not," said Moscow merrily. "What a silly old fool you are! Goodbye, and thank you."

"Where may I kiss you, on the cheek or the hand?"

"Cheeks and hands are forbidden," laughed Moscow. "Lips are allowed. But let me do the kissing!"

She kissed him and went. The man was left to settle the bill without her, astonished at the heartlessness of the young generation, who kiss passionately, as if they're in love, when really they're saying goodbye for ever.

She walked alone through the dawn capital. Her walk was

so self-important, so mocking, that the yardmen all turned their hoses away, and not one drop of water fell on Moscow's dress.

Her life was still long, what stretched out ahead of her was almost immortality. Nothing frightened her heart, and somewhere in the distance, ready to defend her youth and her freedom, cannons were dozing, the way a thunderstorm sleeps in the clouds during winter. Moscow looked at the sky; the wind was moving about like a living being, stirring the murky mist that humanity had breathed up during the night.

On Kalanchevskaya Square, behind the plank fence surrounding the excavations, the compressors of the Metropolitan railway were snorting away. A placard hung by the workers' entrance: KOMSOMOLETS, KOMSOMOLKA! HELP BUILD THE METRO![21] YOUR FUTURE WORLD NEEDS A GREAT RAILWAY!

Moscow Chestnova believed, and went in through the gates; she wanted to take part in everything and she was filled by that indeterminacy of life which is just as happy as its definitive resolution.

10

SARTORIUS HAD SOLVED THE PROBLEM OF SCALES FOR the collective farms. He had thought up a method of weighing grain on a piece of quartz. The stone was quite small, only a few grams. Under compression from load bearing, it emitted a weak electric charge; this charge, amplified by radio valves, then moved a needle that registered the weight on a dial. There were radios everywhere – at grain collection stations, in the homes of collective farm workers and in clubs – and so the new scales consisted simply of a wooden platform, a piece of quartz and a dial, thus being three times cheaper than the old scales and not needing any iron.

Sartorius was now converting to electricity the whole of the Republic's stock of scales. He wanted to replace the world's passive constant – the gravity of the earth – with an active constant – the energy of an electrical field. This would make the machines cheaper, as well as giving them a sharp sense of accuracy.

Summer came to an end and the rains began, as long and as dismal as in early childhood in the days of capitalism. Sartorius seldom went home; he was afraid of being on his own with the yearning he felt for his beloved, vanished Moscow. And so he worked at his plans with zealous concentration, and his heart calmed down, aware of the benefit, both to the State and to the collective farm workers, of the millions of roubles that would be saved by technical improvements to the State's stock of scales. Here, in the Old Merchants' Arcade, in an institute linked to an impoverished and half-forgotten industry, Sartorius found not only recognition for his labour but also human consolation in his sorrow.

Viktor Vasilievich Bozhko, the former chairman of the trade union committee of the Institute for Scales, Weights and Measures, had learned Sartorius's secret. As usual Sartorius had been working late into the evening. There was no one there except an accountant, who was drawing up the quarterly balance, and Bozhko, who was some way away, putting up a new edition of the wall newspaper. Sartorius was staring out of the window: whole crowds of people were travelling by in trams, on their way home from theatres and from visiting their friends. They felt merry in one another's company and could count on their lives getting better, though the technology beneath them was straining – the springs of the tram-cars were buckling and the motors were throbbing exhaustedly.

Sartorius bent down over his work with still greater concern. He needed to resolve not only the problem of balances, but also questions of railway transport and of the passage of ships through the Arctic Ocean; he also had to try to discover the inner mechanical law in a human being that brings about happiness, suffering and death. Sambikin had been wrong to locate the soul of a dead citizen in the emptiness of the intestines, between the excrement and the new intake of food. The intestines were like the brain; their sucking feeling was entirely rational, and it yielded to satisfaction. If the passions of life were concentrated entirely in the darkness of the intestines, world history would not have been so long and all-but fruitless; universal existence, were it founded simply on the law of the stomach, would long ago have become splendid. No, it was not only the dark void of the intestines that had governed the entire world during past millennia, but something different and worse, something more hidden and shameful, beside which all the howling of the stomach seems touching and justified, like the sorrow of a child. But this other thing had never made its way into the mind and so it had never before been possible to understand it: only what was similar to consciousness, only something resembling thought itself, could ever find a way into consciousness. But now! – now it was essential to understand everything, because either socialism would succeed in penetrating into the most secret recess of a man's insides and cleaning out the pus that capitalism had accumulated drop by drop over the centuries, or else nothing new would happen and the inhabitants of the earth would each go off to live separately, keeping this terrible secret place of the soul safe and warm inside them, so as to sink their teeth into each other once again in voluptuous despair and transform the earth's surface into a lonely desert with one last weeping human being.

"What a lot of work there is to do!" Sartorius said out loud. "Don't come, Moscow, I haven't got time now."

At midnight Bozhko boiled some water with an electric element and courteously offered a glass of tea to Sartorius. He sincerely respected the hard-working young engineer who had willingly come to work for an unknown industry of little importance, turning his back on the glories of aviation, super-fast transport and the decomposition of the atom. They drank tea and talked about how to eliminate defects from the manufacture of weights, about Point 21 in the regulations for the verification of measuring instruments, and other such apparently boring matters. But behind all this lay the passion of Bozhko's entire heart, since precise weights brought with them a measure of well-being for collective-farm families, and this helped the dawn of socialism, ultimately bringing hope to the souls of all the dispossessed of the globe. A weight, of course, was hardly a matter of great consequence, but then Bozhko did not see himself as being of any great consequence either, and so there was always enough raw material for his happiness.

The capital was going to sleep. There was only the far-off tapping of a typewriter in some late office and the sound of steam being let off from the chimneys of the Central Power Station. Most people were now lying down, resting or embracing; or else, in the darkness of their rooms, they were feeding on the secretions and secrets of their hidden souls, on the dark ideas of egotism and illusory bliss.

"It's late," said Sartorius, finishing his tea. "Everyone in Moscow's already asleep. It's probably only scum who are still awake – lusting and yearning."

"Who do you mean, Semyon Alekseevich?" asked Bozhko.

"People who have a soul."

Bozhko wanted to answer, out of politeness, but he said nothing, not knowing what to say.

"But everyone has a soul," Sartorius went on morosely. In exhaustion, he laid his head on the desk. Everything seemed dismal and hateful. Night went on, as wearisome as the monotonous knocking of a heart in an unhappy chest.

"Has it really been established with certainty that the soul is universal?" asked Bozhko.

"No, not with certainty," Sartorius answered. "The soul is still unknown."

Sartorius fell silent; his mind had tensed in the struggle against his narrow, poverty-stricken feelings and their incessant love for Moscow Chestnova, and the rest of the varied world was now present for him only in a weak light of consciousness.

"Can't we hurry up and find out what the soul really is?" asked

Bozhko. "It's true: we must remake the whole world and make everything splendid. Think of all the filth that has seeped into humanity during the thousands of years we've been like animals! Something's got to be done with it all. Even our body's not the way it should be – it's full of dirt."

"It certainly is," said Sartorius.

"When I was young," Bozhko went on, "I often wanted everyone to die all at once and I'd wake up in the morning and find I was on my own. But everything else was going to stay the same: the food, and all the buildings – and one lonely, beautiful girl who wouldn't die either, and we'd meet and never part."

Sartorius looked at him with sorrow: how alike we all are – one and the same pus flows in all our bodies!

"That's what I thought too, when I was in love."

"Who was the woman, Semyon Alekseevich?"

"Moscow Chestnova."

"Ah, her!" Bozhko mouthed soundlessly.

"Did you know her too?"

"Only very slightly, Semyon Alekseevich, only vaguely. I wasn't important to her."

"Never mind," said Sartorius, remembering himself. "Now we're going to intervene in what lies inside a man, we're going to find his poor, terrible soul."[22]

"It's time we did, Semyon Alekseevich," said Bozhko. "Somehow I've had enough of being the old kind of natural man. My heart's sick of it all. Mother History's made monsters of the lot of us!"

Bozhko made a bed for Sartorius in the director's armchair, and himself lay down to sleep on the desk. He was now even more content: the very best engineers had begun to think about remodelling the inner soul. For a long time he had secretly feared for communism: might it not be defiled by the alien spirit constantly rising up from the lowest depths of the human organism? After all, ancient, long-lasting evil had eaten deep into the flesh of life, even the human body itself was probably just one solid, all-enduring ulcer – or else it was some downright fraud that had deliberately cut itself off from the entire world in order to conquer it and devour it in solitude.

In the morning, when he woke up, Bozhko saw that Sartorius had not lain down at all. He had prepared a whole file of diagrams and calculations for the country's stock of electric scales; yet there were dried-up traces of tears on his face, as well as the lines left by his struggle against the obsessive despair of yearning feelings.

Bozhko arranged that the presidium of the trade union committee should meet that evening. He tactfully informed them of the personal grief of engineer Sartorius and outlined measures for the reduction of his suffering. "Our usual practice is to intervene only in broad and general matters," he said, "but we must also try to be of help in matters that are deep and personal. Think about it, comrades, as Soviet citizens and as human beings! You remember how Stalin carried the urn with the ashes of engineer Fedoseenko.[23] Although comrade Sartorius's grief is not ordinary, because of the depth of his feeling, it must be comforted by ordinary measures, since in life, as I have observed – though perhaps inaccurately – it is ordinary things that are most powerful of all. That, at least, is how it seems to me."

Lisa the typist, a member of the trade union committee, secretly began to love Sartorius, with credulous willingness. Then, however, she felt ashamed. She was a tender and indecisive woman; her face nearly always had a pink flush from the conscientious tension she felt with other people. A virgin, she was filling out early, her dark hair was growing thicker and thicker, and she had come to look so attractive that a lot of men now noticed her and imagined her as their personal happiness. Sartorius alone had no thoughts about her, and was only vaguely aware of her.

Two days later Bozhko advised Sartorius to look again at Lisa. "She's very sweet and kind," he said, "but her modesty makes her unhappy."

In time, as they worked together, Sartorius got to know Lisa better; and once, in bewilderment, not knowing what to say, he stroked her hand as it lay on the typing table. Lisa left her hand where it was, and said nothing. It was evening; quick as time itself, the moon was climbing into the sky behind the institute walls, as if registering how, minute by minute, youth was draining away.

Lisa and Sartorius went out together onto the street, which had been taken over by such a dense toing and froing of people that one might have thought it was there that society reproduced and multiplied. They rode in a tram to the outskirts of the city. It was already late autumn, a cold dryness lay over the tussocky fields, and the rye that had once grown there, lit by the dawnlike glow of the midnight city, had now been harvested, leaving the place desolate. Filled with terror by his memories, Sartorius embraced Lisa, looking out into the solitary dark of the night around him; Lisa clung to him in response, keeping herself warm and appropriating him with her hands, like a sensible housewife.

After this, Sartorius found comfort for his soul in the institute, and his dreary ache for Moscow Chestnova changed into a sad memory of her, as though she had died. He received a considerable amount of money for the quartz scales, and with this money he dressed Lisa in luxury. For some time he lived lightheartedly, even merrily, devoting himself to love, theatre-going, and pleasures of the moment. Lisa was faithful to him and happy, her only fear being that Sartorius might leave her; as he slept, she would look at his face for a long time, wondering if there were some way she could secretly and painlessly spoil his appearance, even though he was already far from hand-some – he would then be so very ugly that no other woman would love him and he would stay with her right up until death. But Lisa couldn't think of anything; she didn't know what to do to make Sartorius seem loathsome to the entire world – and when he smiled in his sleep at some unknown pleasing dream, her eyes filled with tears of jealous grief and emerging fury.

Sartorius's mind calmed down. Like seeds in a seed-vessel, thoughts and fantasies appeared in him of their own accord, and he would wake up full of discoveries and far-flung ideas. He would imagine the impoverished provinces of southern, soviet China, or Malmgren, the Swedish scientist the world had forgotten, who had frozen to death in the northern ice. And, unsettled by the responsibility of his life, terrified by its speed, frivolity and illusory fulfilment, Sartorius worked with increasing haste, afraid of dying or falling in love with Moscow Chestnova again and going through torment.

Winter set in. Often Sartorius worked all night long in the institute, while Lisa typed away in a far corner. He came up with an idea for electrical scales that would weigh the stars at a distance, as they first appeared over the eastern horizon. For this he received a kiss from the Deputy People's Commissar for Heavy Industry. Gradually, however, Sartorius lost interest in both scales and stars: inside him he felt a confused agitation, something more than could be explained by the high spirits of youth,

II

THAT WINTER, AFTER AN ALARM SIGNAL AT TWO o'clock in the morning, the lift was put into operation in shaft number 18 of the Moscow Metropolitan Construction Project; a young female worker was brought to the surface and an ambulance was summoned. The young woman's leg had been crushed – the full, upper part of her right leg, above the knee.

"Are you in a lot of pain?" asked the foreman. He was leaning over her, grey with exhaustion and fear.

"Of course I am, but it's nothing terrible!" the young worker replied in a sensible voice. "Maybe I'll be able to stand up in a moment."

And she got up from the stretcher, walked a few steps, and fell down in the snow. Blood came out of her; the snow was lit by a searchlight and on it the blood seemed yellow, as if it had been exhausted while still inside her body, but the fallen woman's face was looking up with shining eyes, and her lips were red with health or from a high temperature.

"How on earth did this happen?" the foreman asked as he helped her back onto the stretcher.

"I can't remember," answered the wounded woman. "Some trucks jumped out at me and I was trapped in a dead end and they crushed me. But go away now – I want to sleep, I don't want to feel this pain."

The foreman left, ready to tear off one of his own legs, if only the young woman could survive in one piece. A car came and took the now sleeping worker to the surgical clinic.

Sambikin was the doctor on night duty in the experimental

clinic. No urgent cases had been brought in, so he was sitting on his own with some dead matter, trying to extract the little-known, merry substance which had been stored up inside it, ready for a long life that had failed to happen.

Before Sambikin, on the experiment table, lay the boy he had operated on. He had lain ill in hospital for a long time but had died the previous day, and for a short period before his death he had been demented: pus had appeared in the site of the operation, in the cavities of the bones of his head, and this pus had instantly, quick as fire, poisoned his consciousness. The nurse told Sambikin how, before the little patient momentarily closed his eyes, they had been calm and full; but when he opened his eyes again, they were dull and empty, as if something had pierced right through them.

In long solitude Sambikin had stroked the naked body of the dead child – the most sacred property of socialism – and grief had warmed up inside him, a desolate grief that could never be salved.

Towards midnight, using his instruments, he had dug out the heart from the dead boy's chest; then he had removed a gland from the area of the throat and had begun to investigate these two organs with his devices and preparations, so as to find out where the unspent charge of living energy was being stored. Sambikin was convinced that life was only one of the rare peculiarities of eternally dead matter, and that this peculiarity was concealed where matter was most durably structured; this was why the dead needed as little, to come back to life, as they had previously needed in order to die. More than that, the vital tension of someone being consumed by death was so great that a sick person is sometimes stronger than a healthy one, while the dead may have more potential for life than the living.

Sambikin had decided to use the dead to revive the dead,[24] but then he was called to a woman who was wounded but alive.

The woman from the shaft had been laid on the dressing station, her face covered by a double layer of muslin. She was asleep.

Sambikin examined her leg. Blood was coming out under pressure, and slightly foaming; the bone was shattered along its whole length and all kinds of filth were embedded in the wound. But the surrounding intact body looked gentle and tanned, and the curves of late innocence were so fresh and full that this worker surely deserved immortality; even the strong smell of sweat given off by her skin brought with it a charm, an excitement of life, that made one think of bread and of wide expanses of grass.

Sambikin gave orders for the mutilated woman to be made ready, so he could operate when it was day.

In the morning Sambikin saw that it was Moscow Chestnova on the operating table; she was conscious and she greeted him, but her leg had gone dark and the veins, filled with dead blood, had swollen up like the varicose veins of an old woman. Moscow had been washed, and her pubic hair shaved.

"Well then, goodbye!" said Sambikin, wiping his large hands.

"Goodbye!" Moscow replied – and her eyes began to wander, because she had inhaled a sleeping substance given to her by the nurse.

She lost consciousness and began to move her rustling lips in the thirst of a hot body.

"She's asleep," said the nurse, laying bare all of Moscow.

Sambikin worked on the leg for a long time, eventually taking it right off in order to save the organism from gangrene. Moscow lay there peacefully. A sad, indefinite dream was floating in her consciousness. She was running down a street where both animals and people lived. The animals were tearing off pieces of her body and eating them; the people were clawing at her and trying to hold her back, but she went on running, away from them, down towards an empty sea where someone was weeping for her. Her torso was growing smaller every minute, her clothes had been torn off long ago; in the end there was nothing left but protruding bones, then even these bones were being broken off by passing children, but Moscow, sensing that she was thin and getting smaller and smaller, patiently kept on running – anything not to return to the terrible place she had run away from, anything to survive, even if only as a worthless creature composed of a few dry bones . . . She fell against hard stones – and the people and animals that had torn at her as she fled, that had been eating her, fell on her with all their weight.

Moscow woke up. Sambikin was leaning over her and hugging her, smearing her breasts, her neck and her belly with blood.

"Water!" said Moscow.

There was no one else in the operating theatre. Sambikin had long ago sent away the nurses who had been assisting him. From some distant corner came the hissing of a gas stove.

"Now I'm lame," said Moscow.

"Yes," said Sambikin, not letting go of her. "But it makes no difference. I don't know what to say to you . . ."

He kissed her on the mouth. From it came a suffocating smell of chlorine, but Sambikin could now breathe in anything that Moscow breathed out of herself.

"Wait," said Moscow. "I'm ill."

"Forgive me," said Sambikin, moving away from her. "There are things that destroy everything – and you're one of them. When I saw you, I forgot how to think. I thought I would die."

"All right," Moscow said with a faint smile. "Show me my leg."

"It's not here. I've had it sent to my home."

"Why? I'm not a leg."

"What are you then?"

"Not a leg, not breasts, not a belly, not eyes – I don't know what I am. Take me somewhere to sleep."

The next day Moscow's condition deteriorated; she became feverish and there was blood in her urine. Sambikin banged himself on the head – to bring himself back to his senses from the anguish of love – and analysed his own state both physiologically and psychologically. He laughed, exaggeratedly creasing his face, but he could achieve nothing. The bustle and tension of work forsook him; he wandered about as though he had nothing to do, walking alone down distant streets, occupied by love's tedious, unchanging thoughts. Sometimes he leaned his head against a tree on a night-time boulevard, feeling unbearable grief; occasional tears made their way down his face and, feeling ashamed, he would lick them up from around his mouth and swallow them.

During the second night Sambikin took the dead boy's heart and a gland from his neck, prepared a mysterious liquid from them, and injected it into Moscow's body. As he was hardly able to sleep at all now, he wandered about the town until dawn, and in the morning he found the mother of the dead boy in the clinic; she had come to take her son to be buried. Sambikin set off with her, to help her through the necessary formalities – and that afternoon saw him walking beside the thin, trembling woman, following the cart where the boy with the empty chest lay in a coffin. An unknown, strange life opened out before him, a life of grief and the heart, of memories, of the need for comfort and affection. This life was as great as the life of the mind and of diligent work, only more mute.

Moscow Chestnova took a long time to recover; she turned sallow, and her arms wasted away from lack of exercise. But through the window she could see the bare, thin branches of some tree in the hospital yard. All through the long March nights these branches scraped against the window pane, shivering and yearning, sensing that it was time for warmth to set in. Moscow listened to the movement of the moist wind and the branches, tapped her finger against the glass in answer and refused to believe there was anything poor and unhappy in the world – it just wasn't possible! "Soon I'll come out and join you!" she whispered to the world outside, pressing her mouth to the glass.

One April evening, when it was time to go to bed in the clinic, Moscow heard the sound of a fiddle somewhere in the distance. She listened more closely and recognized the music – it was the fiddler from the nearby housing co-operative where Komyagin lived. Time, life and the weather all change; Spring was on its way now, and the musician was playing even better than before. Moscow listened, and pictured to herself the nocturnal gullies out in the fields, and birds in their need flying onward through the cold dark.

In the afternoons Moscow was often visited by friends from her past work down in the earth. After the operation the Metropolitan Works Triangle[25] had twice been to see her, bringing her cakes in boxes – a gift from the trade union.

"When I get better, I'll marry Komyagin," Moscow would think at night, listening to the fiddler's music as it spread through the vast air. "I'm lame now – I'm a lame woman!"

She was discharged at the end of April. Sambikin brought her some sturdy new crutches – for the whole of the long journey of her remaining life. But there was nowhere for Moscow to go; before the hospital she had lived with everyone else in Metro Works Hostel no. 45, but the hostel had moved and Moscow had no idea where it was now.

Sambikin opened the car door and waited for an address to take her to, but Moscow smiled and said nothing. Sambikin took her to his own home.

A few days later, without waiting till the wound on Moscow's leg had fully healed, Sambikin set off with her to the Caucasus, to a sanatorium beside the Black Sea.

Every morning, after breakfast, Sambikin would accompany Moscow to the shore of the noisy sea and she would look for hours into irrevocable space. "I'll go away, I'll go away somewhere," she would whisper repeatedly. Sambikin would remain silent beside her, his insides aching as though they were slowly rotting, while one and the same beggarly thought – of love for Moscow's impoverished, one-legged body – languished inside his now empty head. Sambikin was ashamed of having such a pitiful life; in the dead hours after lunch he would walk to a little wood in the hills and mutter to himself, breaking off branches, singing and begging the whole of nature to leave him alone and finally grant him peace and the ability to work; he would then lie down on the earth and sense how uninteresting all of this was.

When he came back in the evening, Sambikin often found he couldn't even get near Moscow, so surrounded was she by the attentions, care and persistence of the men – who were putting on weight as they holidayed. It was now barely noticeable that Moscow was crippled; a prosthesis had been brought for her from Tuapse and she was walking without crutches, just with the help of a stick – on which her admirers had already carved their names and the date, together with symbols of noble passions. When she examined this stick, Moscow would think that, if these etchings were sincerely meant, she would have to go and hang herself, for every one of these men was saying the same thing: that he wanted her to bear his children.

Once Moscow had a desire for grapes, but grapes don't grow in Spring. Sambikin went round the nearby collective farms, but found that all the grapes had long been made into wine. Moscow felt distressed; since her illness and the loss of her leg she had been seized by all kinds of whims, getting impatient over things that were quite trivial. She washed her hair every day, for example, because she constantly felt there was dirt in it, and she would even cry from distress, because the dirt just wouldn't go away. One evening, when Moscow was in the garden, washing her hair over a bowl as usual, an elderly man from the mountains came up to the fence and silently began to watch.

"Grandpa, go and fetch me some grapes!" Moscow asked him. "Or haven't you got any?"

"I haven't," replied the man from the mountains. "Where would I get grapes from at this time of year?"

"Well, don't look at me then!" said Moscow. "Have you really not got a single grape? Can't you see – I'm lame!"

The man went off without an answer, but Moscow saw him again the following morning. He waited for her to come out onto the main porch and then gave her a new basket; beneath fresh leaves lay carefully selected grapes, more than a *pood*[26] of them. Then the man from the mountains gave Moscow something very small, a scrap of coloured cloth. Moscow unwrapped it and found a nail from a human big-toe. She did not understand.

"Take it, my Russian lass," the old peasant explained. "I'm 60 years old, that's why I'm giving you my nail. If I were 40, I'd be bringing you my toe, and if I were 30, I'd have torn off my own leg, the leg you don't have."

Moscow frowned, so as to keep her joy calmly in check, but then turned round to run away, and fell, knocking the lifeless wood of her leg against the stone of the threshold.

The man from the mountains did not want to know all there was to know about a person, but only what was best, so he went straight back to his hut and never appeared again.

The time of rest and healing came to an end. Moscow had fully recovered and now used her wooden leg as though it were a living one. As before, Sambikin accompanied her every day to the shore, then left her there on her own.

The movement of water in space reminded Moscow Chestnova of the great destiny of her life: the world really was infinite and there was nowhere its ends would ever meet – a human being is irrevocable.

By the day of their return journey Sambikin's love for Moscow had been transformed for him into such an intellectual riddle that he began to devote the whole of himself to its solution, forgetting the feeling of suffering in his heart.

12

SARTORIUS WAS NO LONGER AN ENGINEER OF NATION-WIDE renown; he was now entirely devoted to the affairs of a little-known institute and he had been gradually forgotten both by former comrades and by more famous organizations. He went home less and less often in the evenings, staying all night in his workplace instead; as a result, in accordance with the rules of residency, his name was struck off the house register and his belongings were taken to a cell in the local police station. Swallowed up by his mute life, Sartorius collected his things, then threw them down in the corner where the night watchman usually dozed in his struggle against possible theft. From then on the institute well and truly became Sartorius's family, refuge and new world. He lived there with his faithful young Lisa and had many friends among his fellow-workers; and the trade union committee, headed by Bozhko, protected him from all grief and unhappiness.

In the daytime Sartorius was nearly always happy, satisfied by the work he was doing, but during the nights, as he lay on his back on heaps of old files, *toskà* was born inside him, a restless yearning that grew up from beneath the bones of his chest like the tree that climbed towards the vaulted ceiling of the Old Merchants' Arcade and rustled its black leaves there. As Sartorius hardly knew how to dream, all he could do was suffer, and observe what was going on.

His mind grew poorer and poorer, his back grew weak from his work, but Sartorius patiently put up with himself; only now and then did his heart ache – insistently and for a long time, in the remote depths of his body, resounding there like a dark wailing voice. Then he would retire behind the cupboard with the old files and stand there for a while in the space between items of stock, waiting for the aching dismalness of his feelings to pass away in solitude and monotony.

At night Sartorius slept little. He would pay visits to the family of Lisa the typist, drink tea with her and her little old mother – who loved to talk about contemporary literature, and especially about paths of development in the visual arts – and smile meekly out of despair. Sometimes Viktor Vasilievich Bozhko would come too. Once, before the appearance of Sartorius, Lisa had been seen as Bozhko's intended; Bozhko, however, having got caught up in institute matters and everyday life with his colleagues, had seen no acute need yet to shut himself away in a conjugal room, and had himself prompted Lisa to console Sartorius. For Bozhko, service to a colleague, and this colleague's happiness, eclipsed the heart and its elemental passions, and the hearth that warmed his personal soul was the Institute for Weights and Measures. When he found Sartorius and Lisa with the little old woman they all shared, Bozhko would diligently apply himself to encouraging them to marry; it delighted him to see young people who were in love remaining in the same institute and trade union, never leaving the small, close-knit system of the weights and measures industry.

If Sartorius did not visit Lisa, he would walk for miles round the city, spend a long time in shops observing bread and vegetables being weighed on electrical scales of his own design, and sigh at the dreary process of unchanging existence enclosed within him. Later, as the empty trams of the night rushed by on their last journeys, Sartorius would stare for a long time into the strange, incomprehensible faces of the few passengers. Some-where or other he was expecting to see Moscow Chestnova, her sweet hair hanging down through the wide-open window of a tram while her head lay on the sill and slept in the wind of movement.

He loved her constantly. The sound of her voice was always there, in the air close by him; he needed only to recall a single word of hers and he would immediately see in his memory her familiar mouth, her loyal, frowning eyes, and the warmth of her gentle lips. Sometimes she would appear in his dreams – wretched, or already dead, lying in poverty on the eve of her burial. Sartorius would wake up in grief and bitterness and immediately busy himself with some useful task in his institute, to eclipse this thought inside him that was so sad and wrong. Usually, though, he did not dream at all, not possessing the capacity for empty experience.

For many months time passed almost unchangingly, with only small variations. The women had long been wearing their warm hats, the skating rinks had opened, the trees on the boule-vards had gone to sleep, preserving the snow on their branches until Spring, the power stations were working more and more strenuously, lighting up the growing darkness, but Moscow Chestnova was nowhere to be found – neither in the world outside, nor in answers to Sartorius's enquiries at the Bureau of Addresses.

In the middle of one winter day Sartorius visited Doctor Sambikin. Sambikin had come back from night work in the clinic and was sitting there quite still, observing the passage through his mind of a current problem.

Strange to say, after not seeing one another for some time, the two friends met without joy, although Sambikin, in his usual way, read great significance into Sartorius's visit. It was a new problem for him to puzzle over.

Sambikin, it turned out, had been crazily in love with Moscow and had distanced himself from her consciously, so he could stand aside and resolve the whole problem of love in its entirety: love was too serious a task, it was inadmissible to fling oneself head first into something so unknown. Only afterwards, when his question about his feelings had been clarified, did Sambikin intend to meet Moscow again, in order to live out with her the remnant of time until death and cremation.

"She's lame now," Sambikin went on, "and she lives in the room of comrade Komyagin, a member of the volunteer militia. And her surname is no longer Chestnova."

"Why did you leave her lame and alone?" asked Sartorius. "You loved her."

Sambikin expressed great surprise. "It would be strange if I were to love just one woman when there's a whole billion women in the world and some of them are sure to be even lovelier. Before we can go any further, this question needs a precise answer. What we have here is an evident misunderstanding on the part of the human heart – and nothing more."

After asking for Moscow's address, Sartorius left Sambikin on his own. The doctor did not show Sartorius to the door, but went on sitting there, entirely taken up by thoughts about all of humanity's most important tasks, wishing for world-wide clarity and agreement on every aspect of happiness and suffering.

In the evening Semyon Sartorius went to the Bauman district, and into the yard of the housing co-operative where Komyagin lived. On the other side of the fence the Institute for Experimental Medicine was now completed, and it was lit up by the

pure light of electricity. By the entrance to the house management committee sat an old beggar with a bald head; his hat
was on the ground, empty side up, and across it lay the bow to
his fiddle. Sartorius put some money in the hat and asked the
beggar why his bow was lying idle.

"It's my sign," said the old man. "It's not alms I'm collecting,
but my pension. I've made music here in Moscow all my life,
with ecstasy. Every generation has listened to me with pleasure.
Now let them give me money for food – it isn't time for my
death yet!"

"But why beg?" said Sartorius. "You could be playing your
fiddle."

"I can't," said the old man. "My hands tremble from the
agitation of weakness. And that's not good for art. I can be a
beggar – but I can't be a botcher!"

The long corridor of the old building still smelled of the
enduring remnants of iodine and bleach. During the Civil War
the building had probably been a hospital, with Red Army
soldiers lying in it. Now it was occupied by tenants.

Sartorius went up to Komyagin's door. Behind it he could
hear the quiet voice of Moscow Chestnova. She was probably
lying in bed, talking to the man she now lived with.

"Remember what I told you – how when I was a child I saw
a dark man with a burning torch? He was running down the
street. It was a dark autumn night and the sky was so low there
was no room to breathe."

"Yes I do remember," said a man's voice. "I've already told
you – I was running to confront the enemy. It was me!"

"It was an old man," said Moscow with sad doubt.

"So what? When you have the eyes of a little girl, a 16-
year-old can seem quite elderly."

"That's true," Moscow admitted. Her voice was a little sly, a little sad, as if all this were happening in the nineteenth century, in a large apartment, and she were a woman in her forties. "And now you're all burned out and charred."

"You're quite right, Musya," said Komyagin, calling her by a short form of her name. "I'm vanishing. I'm an old song. My itinerary's nearing its end. Soon I shall collapse into the hollow of personal death."

Musya was silent for a while, and then said: "And the bird that sang your song flew away long ago to warmer lands. You're pathetic. You're no longer a man!"

"I'm worn out," said Komyagin. "Everything's clear. There's only one thing I love now – a bit of law and order in our Republic."

Moscow gave one of her gentle laughs. "Second-class reserve rank and file! How did I manage to find a man like you among such vast masses?"

"The world's not so very big," Komyagin explained. "This is something I've given real thought to, and on two occasions. If you look at a globe or a map, there seems to be lots of everything, but there isn't really. And it's all been taken stock of and noted down. In half an hour you can run your eyes down the entire register of the territory and the population – names, patronymics, surnames and main biographical data!"

The light went out in the corridor thanks to the advent of some maximal time of night and careful supervision by the comrade responsible for energy. Sartorius leaned his head against the cold sewage pipe that Moscow had once embraced and heard the intermittent sound of filth flowing down from the upper floors.

"And it's a good thing the earth's not that big. You can live a quiet life on it!" Komyagin went on.

Musya-Moscow said nothing. Then came the knock of her wooden leg. Sartorius realized she had sat up.

"Komyagin, were you really a Bolshevik?" she asked.

"Never! Certainly not! Why?"

"Then why were you running with a torch in 1917, when I was still growing?"

"I had to," said Komyagin. "There was no militia then – and certainly no volunteer militia. People had to be their own self-defence against every enemy."

"But where we lived – and you too – nearly everyone was begging or starving. My father had three roubles' worth of property – and you'd have had to tear it off his back and out of his belly. What were you guarding, you fools? Why were you running with a torch?"

"I was an inspector of self-defence. I was running to check the guard-posts. When there's very little of everything, that means poverty. And poverty needs all the more protection – it's what's most precious of all. A wooden spoon turns into a silver spoon. It really does!"

"But who fired that shot and started all the shouting in the prison? Don't lie to me!"

"What do you mean – lie? The truth's even worse. The man who fired the shot was a solitary hooligan. And what was going on in the prison was a meeting – elections to a constituent assembly.[27] They were well fed in there and no one wanted to leave and be free. They had to be driven out into freedom by force. I had some cabbage soup there myself – I knew one of the warders."

Moscow slowly took off her clothes, breathing heavily and shuffling her wooden leg. She was probably settling down for the night.

Sartorius waited in fear of further developments. Now and again tenants would go down the corridor to the communal toilet, but they paid no particular attention to the unknown human being in the darkness, as though they were already accustomed to every kind of incomprehensible phenomenon.

"Blind man in the nettles!" said Moscow behind the door. "Don't you lie down with me, you filth!"

"Creak away, peg-leg!" said Komyagin patiently. "What can you know of the life of a man like me?"

"More than enough! You should be done away with – that's as much as anyone needs to know of your life."

"Wait a minute! I haven't finished a single task yet. I haven't thought through my most important thoughts."

"Maybe you never will. You're getting old. What are you hoping for?"

Komyagin modestly informed her that he was hoping to win several thousand roubles through the State loan scheme. Then he'd rethink all of his thoughts and complete all the tasks he had begun.

"But that may not be for a long time," said Moscow sadly.

"Even if it's only an hour before my death, it'll still give me all the time I need!" Komyagin insisted. "Anyway, even if I don't win, even if I don't make my life into something normal, I've made up my mind! As soon as I sense the approach of my natural end, I'll get down to all my tasks. I'll sort out my thoughts and get everything finished. Just 24 hours or so – that's all I need. Even in one hour you can cope with all of life's tasks! Life's nothing so very special – I've really thought about it and I know what I'm saying. It's not true you need to live 100 years and that you might not complete all your tasks even then. It's not true at all! You can live 40 years to no avail – but if you get down to work an hour before the coffin, you can finish every-thing off very nicely – everything you were born for!"

They did not talk any more. Komyagin – judging from the sounds – lay down on the floor and sighed for a long time, upset that time went on passing yet his affairs never progressed. Sartorius stood there in despondency, without any decision. He heard someone, the last human being up and about, lock the door to the street and retire to their room to sleep. But Sartorius was not afraid of spending the entire night in the darkness of the corridor. He went on waiting: maybe Komyagin would die soon – then he would be able to go into the room himself and be on his own there with Moscow. He stayed awake in expec-tation, observing in the dark silence the gradual passage of a night that was full of events. From behind the third door after the sewage pipe came orderly sounds of copulation; the cistern on the wall of the empty toilet hissed with air, sometimes more loudly, sometimes more softly, testifying to the working of the powerful water-main; far away, at the end of the corridor, a soli-tary tenant shouted out several times in the horror of a dream, but there was no one to comfort him and he began to calm down independently; in the room opposite Komyagin's someone had woken on purpose and was praying to God in a whisper: "Remember me, Lord, in thy kingdom, as I remember thee. And grant me something factual – I beg you!" The other rooms along the corridor also had their events going on in them – events that were trivial but uninterrupted and indispens-able, making the night as charged with life and activity as the day. Sartorius listened and realized how impoverished he was to have only a single torso that was closed in from every side. Moscow and Komyagin were sleeping behind the door; their heart was beating subduedly, and from all along the corridor came the sound of communal, peaceful breathing, as if there were nothing but kindness in the breast of every person.

Sartorius was in anguish. He knocked carefully at the door, wanting someone to wake up and something to happen. Moscow was sleeping lightly, and she turned over and called Komyagin. He replied irritably. What could she be wanting from him at night when he was no use to anyone even in the day?

"Check your State bonds," said Moscow. "Turn on the light."

"What is it?" asked Komyagin in alarm.

"Maybe you've won something. If you have, then you can start living life correctly. But if you haven't, then you can lie down and die. There's no one else like you in the whole of the Soviet Union – you should be ashamed of yourself!"

Komyagin made an effort to gather up the enfeebled thoughts in his head. "The Soviet Union – why are people always going on about the Soviet Union? Nowadays everyone grumbles about it, but I live here without a care in the world!"

"You've done enough living. Now die like a hero," said Moscow, insistently and with venom.

Komyagin reflected. Really, nothing in particular would happen even if he were to die – thousands of millions of souls had already endured death and no one had come back to complain. But life evidently still fettered him with its bones, with its growth of flesh and its networks of veins – the mechanical stability of his own being was something too sure and habitual. He crawled on his knees into his unfinished archives and began going through his bonds, while Moscow read out the list of winning numbers from the People's Commissariat of Finance booklet. One bond turned out to have won ten roubles, but Komyagin owned only a quarter of this successful bond, and so his net profit was just two and a half roubles; his life had been augmented only to an insignificant extent, and it was still impossible to draw up the accounts without their showing a loss.

"So now what?" asked Moscow.

"I shall die," Komyagin agreed. "It's not my lot to go on living. Go to the police station tomorrow and hand in my book of fine-receipts. There'll be a percentage of five roubles for you to collect. You can live on it when I'm gone."

He then lay down on something and fell silent.

Soon afterwards Moscow whispered another question: "Well, Komyagin?" She was calling him by his surname, as if he were a stranger. "Gone back to sleep? And then you'll be waking up again, I suppose?"

"I'm not really asleep," Komyagin answered. "I've been doing some thinking. What if I serve another ten years in the militia? Then I'd really learn how to instil discipline! I could become another Genghis Khan!"

"Stop all this talk!" said Moscow angrily. "You're a cheat! You're stealing time from the State!"

"No, I'm not!" protested Komyagin. He then said with feeling: "Be sweet to me, Musya. Then I'll waste away more quickly. By morning I'll be an angel – I'll have died."

"I'll show you how sweet I can be!" Moscow replied threateningly. "If you don't stop breathing soon, I'll trample you to death with my wooden leg."

"All right, all right! They say that, before one dies, one should recall one's whole life. Don't shout at me – I'll start right now."

Silence set in as long years of existence passed one by one through Komyagin's mind.

"Well, have you done remembering?" said Moscow, hurrying him on.

"There's nothing to remember," said Komyagin. "All I can

think of is the seasons: autumn, winter, spring, summer, and then again autumn, winter . . . In 1911 and 1921 there was a hot summer and a bare winter, without any snow. 1916 was the opposite – it poured with rain. And 1917 had a long, dry autumn – just right for the Revolution. I can remember it as if it were today."

"But you've loved a lot of women, Komyagin. That must have been your happiness."

"What happiness can there be for a man like me? It wasn't happiness – just the poverty of lust! That's all love is – a bitter need."

"You know, Komyagin, you're not so very stupid after all!"

"Just average," agreed Komyagin.

"All right then," said Moscow in a clear voice. "That's enough!"

"All right," Komyagin repeated.

They fell silent again, and for a long time. Behind the door to where they lived, Sartorius waited impassively for Komyagin to die, so he could go into the room himself. He felt his eyes beginning to ache, from the dark and from long anguish of heart.

Eventually Komyagin asked Musya to cover his head up tight with a blanket, and to secure the blanket with a piece of string round his torso, so it wouldn't slip off. Wearing her wooden leg, Moscow got out of bed, covered Komyagin up in the required manner, and then settled back down again, with repeated sighs.

The night stood still, as if stagnant. Sartorius sat down on the ground in exhaustion: no one along the corridor had woken up yet, morning was still somewhere over the mirror of the Pacific Ocean. But every sound had stopped, events had evidently made their way deep into the sleepers' bodies; only the pendulums of the wall-clocks were knocking away for all to hear, as if some very important production mechanism were at work. And the work of the pendulums truly was of great importance; they were propelling forward the time that had accumulated, so that both heavy and happy feelings should pass through a human being without delays, without coming to a stop and destroying him once and for all.

No pendulum was at work in Komyagin's room; all that could be heard from there was the pure, even breathing of Moscow, who was now asleep. There was no other breathing – none that Sartorius could detect. After waiting a little longer, he knocked at the door.

"Who's there?" Moscow asked immediately.

"Me," said Sartorius.

Without getting up, Moscow released the door hook with the big toe of her intact foot.

Sartorius went in. The light was on; it had been burning ever since the checking of the State bonds. Komyagin was lying on the floor, on some bedding, with a thick blanket wrapped tightly round his head; the blanket was held in place by a thin piece of string which cut into his chest. Moscow was alone on the bed, covered by a sheet; she smiled at Sartorius and began chatting to him. After a while Sartorius asked, "How is it you've ended up here, in the room of a stranger? And why?"

Moscow replied that she had hadn't known what to do with herself. At first Sambikin had loved her, but then he had begun to puzzle over her, as if she were some problem, and had stayed continually silent. And she herself had begun to feel ashamed of living among her former friends, in their shared, orderly city, now that she was lame, thin and mentally not right in the head. So she had decided to hide away in the room of someone she knew, someone poor, to wait until time had passed and she could be merry again.

She was sitting on the bed, with Sartorius beside her. After a while she lowered her now pale face; her long dark hair fell forward across her cheeks, and she began to cry inside the thicket of her plaits. Sartorius tried to calm her down by means of embraces, but these meant nothing to her; she felt ashamed and hid her wooden leg deep beneath her skirt.

"Is he asleep?" Sartorius asked, pointing to Komyagin.

"I don't know," said Moscow. "Maybe he's died – it's what he wanted. Feel his feet."

Sartorius felt the tips of Komyagin's feet. The remains of his socks were like neckties – only the upper parts were whole, while Komyagin's toes and the soles of his feet were exposed quite naked. His toes and heels proved to be cold right through to the bone, and his whole body lay in a position of helplessness.

"He's probably died," said Sartorius.

"It's about time he did," said Moscow quietly.

Sartorius silently rejoiced that there was no one alive in the room except for himself and his very same, beloved Moscow, now sweeter and closer to his heart than ever, and that her happiness and fame had temporarily stopped, which meant that everything now lay ahead of her. He felt no pity for Komyagin. The night had been going on for a long time; Sartorius and Moscow were both exhausted and they got onto the bed to lie down side by side.

Komyagin remained motionless far away on the floor. The evening before, so that his bedding wouldn't get dirty, Moscow had spread out some old newspapers, *Izvestiyas* from 1927, and light was now falling on reports of past events. Sartorius embraced Moscow and began to feel happy.

Some two hours later people began to go up and down the corridor, getting ready for office and factory. Sartorius awoke and sat up on the bed. Moscow was asleep beside him, and in her sleep her face was peaceful and kind, like bread, not quite like her usual face. Komyagin was lying there the same as before; the electricity was burning brightly and illuminating the entire room, where everything needed to be remade or else properly finished. Sartorius realized that love came into being as a result of the poverty of society, a universal poverty that had still not been eliminated and which meant people were unable to find any better, higher destiny and didn't know what to do with themselves. He turned out the light and lay down, to recover from the state of mind that had come over him. A weak light, like moonlight, began to spread along the wall above the door, coming in through the window from the morning sky, and when the whole room was lit up, it seemed even sadder, even more cramped than it had done at night, under the electric light.

Sartorius went up to the window. Behind it was the smoky, wintry city; a routine dawn was making its way along the sagging belly of an indifferent cloud from which there was no chance of either wind or storm. But millions of people had begun to stir on the streets, carrying diverse life within them. Amidst the grey light they were on their way to labour in workshops, and to think inside offices and engineering bureaus; there were many of them, while Sartorius was sitting on his own, always inseparable from himself. His mind and soul, together with his monotonous body, had been structured to remain the same until death.

The dead Komyagin lay there, a witness to the events that had happened in the room, but he did not move or feel envious. Moscow was asleep in alienation, her lovely face turned to the wall.

Sartorius suddenly felt frightened: all that had been allotted to him, out of the entire world, was one warm drop stored in his breast, and he would never experience everything else but would soon lie down in a corner like Komyagin. His heart seemed to turn dark but he comforted it, as usual, with an idea that entered his head: that it was necessary to research the entire extent of current life by transforming himself into other people. Sartorius stroked the sides of his body, condemning it to suffer its way into another existence, even though this was forbidden by the laws of nature and the habit people have of staying themselves. Sartorius was a researcher and, rather than preserve himself for secret happiness, he intended to use events and circumstances to destroy the resistance of his personality, so that the unknown feelings of other people could enter him one by one. Since he was here and alive, he must not miss this opportunity. It was essential to enter into every other soul; otherwise what could he do with himself? Alone with himself, there was nothing to live on. And if anyone did live like that, they died long before the coffin.[28]

Sartorius put his face to the window pane, observing the city he loved, and which was growing every minute into the time of the future; excited by work, renouncing itself, it was struggling forward with a face that was young and unrecognizable.

"What good am I on my own? I must become like the city of Moscow."

Komyagin stirred on the floor, and took in a breath of his already well-used air.

"Musya," he called out uncertainly. "I've gone all cold down here. Can I come and lie beside you?"

"Oh, all right!" said Moscow, opening one eye.

Komyagin began to free himself from the blanket that was suffocating him, and Sartorius went out through the door and into the city, without saying goodbye.

13

FOR SOME TIME IT WAS AS IF SARTORIUS WERE NOT living. He stopped going to see Lisa the typist, who was now well and truly married to Bozhko. The Institute for Weights and Measures was now destined for liquidation and had been laid waste, emptied of its staff. Only one woman, the messenger, lived in the now cold and deserted premises; she had given birth to a child, and she nursed him and made a home for him on a soft heap of outdated files.

Sartorius twice visited his old workplace, sat for a while at his bare desk, tried to sketch a machine for weighing something weightless – and felt no sensation at all, neither sorrow nor pleasure. Everything had come to an end: the office family, which had allowed people to unburden their souls, had been dispersed; the communal kettle was no longer put on to boil for twelve o'clock, and the glasses stood empty in the cupboard, where they were gradually colonized by some kind of pale and papery little insect. The messenger's baby cried and was comforted, the pendulum clock up above the baby continued on its way, and the mother caressed her child with the usual love of mothers. She was awaiting with dread the arrival in the building of some new institute, since she had nowhere else to live, but on the eve of the move this new institute was also liquidated, so the space was turned over to the housing reserve and eventually allocated to tenants with families.

Sartorius's sight was growing worse; his eyes were going blind. He lay in his room for a whole month before beginning to see a little again with aching vision. The messenger woman from the old institute came to see him every other day, bringing him food and seeing to the routine chores.

He was twice visited by Sambikin and an eye doctor, and they pronounced their medical diagnosis: that the reason for his eye illness lay in the remote depths of his body, perhaps in his heart. In general, Sartorius's constitution was undergoing a process of indeterminate transformation – a thought Sambikin puzzled over for many days.

Eventually, Sartorius went out of the building. He was gladdened by the crowds on the street. The energy of the rushing cars generated inspiration in his heart; and continual sunlight shone on the uncovered hair of women passing by, and on the fresh leafy leaves of the trees, drenched in the moisture of their birth.

Once again it was Spring; time was bearing Sartorius's life away from him, making it increasingly redundant. He would often blink from being blinded by light, and would bump into people. He was glad there were so many of them and that it was not, therefore, obligatory for him to exist – there were enough people, even without him, to do everything that was essential and worthwhile.

A single heavy, dark feeling had taken hold of him. He carried his body as if it were a dead weight, something sad and boring that he had endured to its wretched end. Sartorius gazed into the many faces he met; another person's life, hidden inside their unknown soul, tormented him like some pale pleasure. He stood aside and yearned.

There were approximately 10,000 people moving about on Kalanchevskaya Square.[29] As if he had never before seen such a sight, Sartorius stopped in astonishment beside the customs house.

"I'll hide away now, I'll disappear among all these people," he said to himself, considering this intention of his lightly and without determination.

A misty figure came up to him, the kind of man you can't remember and always forget.

"Comrade, you don't happen to know where Dominikov Lane begins? Maybe you know it – I used to know it myself, but I've lost the thread."

"Yes," said Sartorius, "it's over there!" And he pointed him in the right direction, remembering the voice, which was familiar to him, but not the face.

"And do you know if coffin production is still going on there – or has it been transferred elsewhere in connection with construction and reorganization?" the passer-by continued.

"I'm not sure. Yes, I think there's something like that – wreaths and coffins."

"And transport?"

"Probably."

"And cars that go slowly and quietly?"

"Could be. They go in first gear and they carry the corpse."

"That's right," the man agreed, not understanding the words *first gear*.

They fell silent. The unknown man looked with passion at some people who were jumping up onto moving trams and clinging to them – and even made a single vague movement of fury in their direction.

"I know you," said Sartorius. "I remember your voice."

"Quite likely," the man said indifferently. "There are a lot of people I've had to fine for infringements, and when you do that, naturally enough, you shout."

"Maybe it'll come back to me. What's your name?"

"First names don't matter," said the man. "What's important is the exact address and the surname – but even that's not enough. One must show one's documents."

He took out his passport, and in it Sartorius read *Komyagin, pensioner*, and the address. The man was a stranger to him.[30]

"We're not acquainted," said Komyagin, seeing Sartorius's disappointment. "You just thought we were. Often something seems important – but really it's nothing at all. Well, you stay here, and I'll go and find out about the coffin."

"Has your wife died?" asked Sartorius.

"No. She's left me. I'm enquiring about the coffin for myself."

"Why?"

"What do you mean – *why*? It's essential. I want to know a deceased person's entire itinerary: where you get authorization for a grave to be dug, what data and documents are needed, how you order the coffin, and then the means of transport, the burial, and how the balance sheet of life is finally drawn up: where and according to what procedures a man is finally excluded from the register of citizens. I want to follow the entire route in advance – from life to complete oblivion, to the absolute liquidation that is the fate of every being. They say this journey is not easy. And it's true, dear comrade, people shouldn't die, there is a need for citizens. But look what's going on in the square! Citizens are rushing about, they just won't learn to walk normally. How often, in his time, did comrade Lunacharsky[31] call for rhythmical movement on the part of the masses – and to this day they still have to be fined! How prosaic life is! Long live the heroic militia of the Republic!"

Komyagin set off towards Dominikov Lane. As well as Sartorius, four passers-by and one vagrant child had been listening to him all agog. This child, aged about twelve, set off briskly after Komyagin and declared in an adult voice, "Citizen, since you're about to go and die anyway, give me your tables and chairs. I'll put new legs on them."

"All right," said Komyagin, "come along with me. You'll inherit my belongings, but I'll carry my share of fate a bit further. Farewell, my life – you have passed by in organizational pleasures."

"It's good of you to be dying," the intelligent child said good-humouredly. "I need resources, you see, for my career."

Sartorius's soul was experiencing the passion of curiosity. He was conscious, as he stood there, of the unavoidable poverty of the separate human heart. For a long time he had been astonished by the spectacle of living people and their diversity; now he wanted to live a life that belonged to someone else and not to him.

He was not under any obligation to return: his room was empty, the institute had been liquidated, his family of colleagues now worked in the well-lived-in rooms of other establishments, Moscow Chestnova was lost somewhere in the space of this city and of humanity – and all this was making Sartorius feel merrier. Life's fundamental obligations – concern for one's personal fate, the sense of one's own body, constantly crying out with feelings – had disappeared. It was impossible for him to remain the same uninterrupted person, he was being gripped by *toskà*.

Sartorius made a movement with his hand – thus, according to the universal theory of the world, instigating an electro-magnetic oscillation which must disturb even the most distant star. He smiled at such a pathetic and impoverished conception of the great world. No, the world was better and more mysterious than that: neither a movement of the hand nor the work of the human heart would disturb the stars – otherwise everything would have been shaken to pieces long ago by all this trembling piffle.

He set off across the square through the oncoming people. He saw a Metro construction worker in overalls, a woman with the same figure as Moscow Chestnova, and his eyes began to ache from the memory of love: it was impossible to live life with feelings that never changed. He tried to persuade the woman into a preliminary friendship, but she laughed and hurried away from him, dirty and beautiful. Sartorius dried his half-blind eyes, and tried to win over his heart, which had begun to ache for Moscow and all other beings, but he realized that his thinking was having no effect. Yet his lack of respect for himself made his suffering less difficult.

As he continued to wander about the city, he often noticed happy, sad or enigmatic faces, and he would wonder who to become. This imagining of other souls, of the unknown sensation of being in a new body, stayed with him. He thought about the thoughts in other people's heads, walked with a gait that was not his own, and felt greedy delight inside his empty and ready heart. For Sartorius, youth of torso was changing into lust of mind; on squares and streets, a modest, smiling Stalin was standing guard over all the open roads of the fresh, unknown, socialist world. Life was stretching out into a distance from which there was no return.

Sartorius caught a tram to the Krestov market, to buy what was necessary for his future existence. His new life was a matter of the utmost concern to him.

The Krestov market was full of trading beggars and secret bourgeois, all of them trying, in dry passions and the risk-taking of despair, to procure their bread. Foul air hung over the crowded gathering of standing, muttering people. Some were proffering

meagre goods, clasping them to their breasts; others were rapa-
ciously asking what these goods cost, prodding them and falling
into despondency, since they had counted on acquiring them for
ever. There were old clothes for sale here, cut in the style of the
nineteenth century, impregnated with powder and kept intact
through decades on a careful body. There were fur coats that had
passed through so many hands during the Revolution that an
entire meridian of the earth would have been too small to
measure their journeys between people. And there were people
trading things which had lost all reason for their existence –
house-coats that had belonged to enormous women, priests'
cassocks, ornamented basins for baptising children, the frock-
coats of deceased gentlemen, charms on waistcoat chains, and so
on – but which still circulated among people as symbols of a strict
evaluation of quality. There were also many items of clothing
worn by people who had died recently – there truly was such
a thing as death – as well as clothes that had been got ready
for children who had been conceived but whose mothers must
have changed their minds about giving birth and had abortions
instead, and now they were selling the tiny wept-over garments
of an unborn child together with a rattle they had bought in
advance.

One row of the market was set aside for reproductions of
famous paintings and original portraits in oil. The portraits
showed long dead burghers, and brides and bridegrooms from
provincial towns; all of them, judging by their faces, took
pleasure in themselves and were satisfied with the life that had
come their way. Behind these figures there was sometimes a
church in open countryside, and the oak-trees of a happy
summer that was always past.

Sartorius stood for a long time in front of these portraits

of past people. Their gravestones were now being used for the pavements of new cities, and somewhere a third or fourth brief generation was trampling over the inscriptions: *Here lies the body of Pyotr Nikodimovich Samofalov, merchant of the second guild of the town of Zaraisk. The years of his life were . . . Remember me, O Lord, in thy kingdom. Here lie the ashes of Anna Vasilievna Strizhevaya, spinster . . . We weep and suffer; but she beholdeth the Lord.*

Rather than God, it was the dead whom Sartorius now remembered, and he shuddered from terror – terror of living among them, in the days before the forests had been cut down, when a man's wretched heart was eternally faithful to solitary feeling, when his circle of acquaintances consisted entirely of relatives, when his vision of the world was patient and magical and his mind languished and wept – by the light of a paraffin lamp in the evening, or during a radiant summer noon – amid a natural world that was spacious and full of noises; a time when a pathetic young girl, devoted and faithful, had embraced a tree in her yearning, a stupid, sweet girl who had now been forgotten without a sound. She was not Moscow Chestnova, but one Ksenia Innokentievna Smirnova, who no longer was, and who never would be again.

Further on, there were sculptures for sale, together with cups, plates, trivets, forks, parts from some balustrade, and a twelve-*pood* weight. The last private traders in hardware were squatting on their haunches; demoralized, out-of-work locksmiths were hawking hammers, vices, axes for firewood, a handful of nails. Further on were cobblers – doing jobs on the spot – and old women selling food: cold pancakes; pies stuffed with butchers' waste; suet buns kept warm in cast-iron pots beneath the padded jackets of the old men, now deceased, who had once been their husbands; slabs of cooked millet; anything, in short, that might relieve the hungry suffering of the local public – who were capable of eating whatever they could swallow, and nothing else.

Petty thieves were wandering about between those who wanted to buy and those who wanted to sell; they would snatch from someone's hands a length of cotton, a pair of old felt boots, some rolls, a single galosh, then run off into the jungle of wandering bodies, earning 50 kopecks or a rouble from each theft. In the end, they barely made as much as a labourer, and exhausted themselves more.

Wooden booths towered up here and there in the market, and policemen looked down from them into this petty sea of raging small-scale imperialism, where there were no labourers any more, only loafers.

The cheap food made an audible noise as it was digested inside people, and so these people felt burdened with heaviness, as if they were complex factories, and unclean air rose up from them, like smoke over the Donbass.[32]

From the depths of the market came frequent shouts of despair, but nobody ever ran to help, and people went on buying and selling in the vicinity of the disaster, because their own grief required urgent consolation. A woman selling rolls had driven a puny man wearing an old army greatcoat into a pool of urine beside the latrines, and she was lashing him across the face with a rag. A wandering hooligan had come to her help, going up to the puny man – who had collapsed beneath the latrine fence – and smashing him in the face till he bled. The man did not cry out and he did not touch his face, now awash with the blood that poured from his temples; hurriedly, struggling with his rotten teeth, he was devouring the stolen dry bun – a task he quickly completed. The hooligan struck him another blow on the head, and the wounded eater, jumping up with the energy of a strength that was incomprehensible in someone so meek and taciturn, disappeared into the thick of the crowd, as if among ears of rye. He would find food for himself everywhere and would live for a long time without means and without happiness, but often eating his fill.

An elderly, demobilised-looking man was standing motionless in one place, just swaying a little from the bustle beside him. Sartorius had noticed him before; he went up to him.

"Ration cards for bread," said the motionless man, after a certain vigilant observation of Sartorius.

"How much?" asked Sartorius.

"Twenty-five roubles, first category."

"I'll have one then," said Sartorius.

The trader cautiously took from a side pocket an envelope with the printed inscription: *Full Programme of the Institute for the Processing of Mineral Resources.* Inside this programme was a ration card.

The same trader also offered Sartorius a passport, should he need one, but Sartorius got himself a passport later, from a man selling worms for bait. The passport was in the name of Ivan Stepanovich Grunyakhin, a 31-year-old native of Novy Oskol, a worker in retailing and the commanding officer of a reserve platoon. Sartorius paid only 65 roubles for the document, handing over at the same time his own passport, that of a 27-year-old man with higher education, well-known among his professional colleagues.[33]

Emerging from out of the market, Grunyakhin didn't know where to go. He went by tram to a large square and then sat down on the iron rung of a ladder that led to a traffic policeman's booth. The traffic lights changed colour, people rushed past in cars, lorries went by with girders and beams, the police-man switched his switch and watched intently: many unknown people were standing on either side of the speeding traffic and forgetting their solitary lives in contemplation of the lives of others. It seemed to Grunyakhin that his eyes no longer ached and that he would never need Moscow Chestnova again, since there were many fine women crossing the road here – yet his heart was not inclined towards any of them.

Towards evening he was taken on by the provisions section of a small factory in Sokolniki[34] that made some kind of auxiliary equipment, and a place was found for the new worker in the hostel, since the man possessed nothing except a small clothed body with a round, stupid-looking face on top of it.

Within a few days Grunyakhin entered into the passion of his work. It was his job to apportion bread for lunch and put the correct quota of vegetables into the pot, and also to work out how much meat each person should be allotted so as to get their fair share. He liked feeding people; he worked with honesty and zeal, and his kitchen scales gleamed with cleanness and precision, like a diesel engine.

In the evenings, wearied by solitude and freedom, Grunyakhin wandered up and down the boulevards until the last trams. After one o'clock in the morning, when the tram-cars were speeding to their depot, Ivan Grunyakhin would climb on board and examine their desolate interiors with interest, as if the thous-ands of people who had been there during the day had left their breath and the best of their feelings on the empty seats. The conductress – sometimes an old woman, sometimes a woman who was young, sweet and sleepy – would be sitting on her own, pulling the cord at the deserted stops, so the last journey would soon be over.

Now that he had become the second person of his life, Grunyakhin would go up to the conductress and begin to talk about something remote, that had nothing to do with all the visible reality around them – and the conductress would then perceive something invisible inside herself. One conductress in the rear car yielded to Grunyakhin's words and he embraced her en route; they then moved to the back of the car, where the light was dimmer, and they went on kissing and were carried away past three stops, until a man on the boulevard noticed them, and called out: "Hurrah!"

After that, he tried now and again to repeat this friendship with a night-time conductress – sometimes succeeding, but more often failing. What most concerned him, however, was not this private love that passed and left no trace, but Grunyakhin, the unknown human being whose fate was swallowing him up.

As he continued with his work in the provisions section, he gradually got excited by this work and by things around him, and even began to feel intoxicated by life. He acquired a bookcase, filled it with books and began studying world philosophy, delighting in universal thought and the fact that good was inevitable in the world, and that it was even impossible for anyone to hide from it. In the end, the laws of the golden rule in mechanics and the golden section in art were valid always and everywhere. It turned out that, thanks to the action of nature alone, a little work would always yield great success and everyone would end up with a piece from the golden section – the grandest and most substantial piece of all. What determined the fate of mankind, therefore, was not labour and diligence but cunning, skill and the soul's readiness to be intoxicated by happiness. Archimedes and Hero of Alexandria had long ago rejoiced in the golden rules of science, which promised widespread bliss to humanity: using a one-gram weight and a lever with arms of unequal length, you could lift a whole ton – even the entire globe of the earth, as Archimedes had calculated. And Lunacharsky, for his part, had proposed lighting a new sun if the present one should come to seem inadequate, or simply tedious and ugly.

Comforted by what he read, Ivan Grunyakhin worked well at the factory. In the course of a month, on instructions from the head of the provisions section, he completely transformed the gloomy decor of the canteen into something luxurious and attractive. He signed a contract for one year with the Green Spaces Board, as well as with MoscFurniture and other organizations. He introduced potted plants and laid down strips of carpet. He then increased the circulation of air and himself repaired an electric motor for the second, damaged extractor fan, recalling his knowledge of electrical engineering with difficulty and no longer feeling any interest in it. On the walls of the canteen and the assembly workshop he hung large pictures of episodes from ancient historical life: the *Fall of Troy*, the *Voyage of the Argonauts*, the *Death of Alexander the Great*. The factory manager praised him for his good taste. "We want things to be mysterious and fine – almost unbelievable," he said to Grunyakhin. "Though of course these paintings are piffle in comparison with our own reality! But let them stay there – history was poor in the past and one shouldn't expect too much from it."

Under the influence of this general well-being and prosperity, Grunyakhin felt suddenly ashamed, and he began to acquire underwear, shoes and fruit for his personal use, and even began to dream of having a one and only loving wife. Sometimes he remembered the poor, long-gone, Institute for Weights and

Measures, when he was still Sartorius. There he had felt a sadness and a warmth that came from his heart, and he had not needed a wife; now, however, having become a different person, Grunyakhin needed at the very least the artificial warming that comes from a family and a woman.

In the workshop of new constructions there was a senior assembly worker, about 30 years old, called Konstantin Arabov; he was handsome, a member of the Dynamo Sports Club, and he knew Pushkin by heart. Duty engineer Ivan Stepanovich Grunyakhin had come across him several times but had never paid any attention to him. It often happens that way – people whose fate will enter right into our heart often go unnoticed for a long time . . . Arabov fell in love with one of the team leaders, a French Komsomol member called Katya Bessonet-Favor,[35] an amusing and intelligent young woman. He went off with her to live in love forever, leaving his wife and two sons – one eleven-year-old, and one eight-year-old. Arabov's wife, still young, but sad, used for a while to go and visit the factory at the end of the day's work, so as to look at her husband; her heart, it seemed, couldn't immediately get used to being without him. Then she stopped going; her feeling of love had reached exhaustion, and it had ended. Soon afterwards Grunyakhin learned from Katya Bessonet that Arabov's eleven-year-old son had shot himself with a neighbour's gun, and had left a note just like a grown-up. Grieving and in tears, Katya told how in a room somewhere a boy had become unhappy and had chosen to die – at a time when she had been intoxicated by happiness with his father. Grunyakhin shuddered from fear and astonishment at such a death, as if somewhere ahead of him he had heard a weak cry amid universal silence. He regretted that he had not known the boy before, that he had overlooked this being.

Tormented by consciousness, Katya Bessonet rejected Arabov, who wanted to calm his despair through still more passionate love with her, as commonly happens. But she was unable to be on her own either; and so she went to the cinema with Grunyakhin, and from there they set off together to visit Arabov's ex-wife. Katya knew that the dead boy's funeral had taken place that morning, and she wanted to help his mother in her eternal separation from the truest, most faithful little person she had known.

Arabov's wife greeted them without emotion. She was clean and well-dressed, as if ready for some modest celebration, and she was calm and not crying. She knew Katya Bessonet, of course, but had only seen Grunyakhin once, at the factory, and did not understand why he had come.

Katya embraced her, but Arabov's wife stood there with her arms hanging down and did not respond; there was nothing that mattered to her now. She mechanically lit the stove and made some tea for these guests who were strangers to her. Grunyakhin liked this woman, with her face that was so ugly and absurd it made you feel sorry for her. Her nose was large and thin, her lips were grey, and her eyes were colourless, muted by the solitary labour of housework; she was not yet old, but her body had already dried up and become like that of a man, and her drooping breasts hung down as if they had nothing to do.

After drinking their tea, the guests got ready to leave. The meeting had not led to consolation, and Katya Bessonet was left with a feeling of irritation inside her from the impotence of her heart, which felt too much but was unable to act. As they left, Arabov's wife suddenly turned towards the emptiness of her room. And Grunyakhin suddenly looked in the same direction himself, and at that moment every object seemed to him to become a likeness, or a distortion, of someone familiar, someone they all knew – and that might even have been his own self; the objects had turned their attention to the people present and were grinning sullenly at them with obscure faces and attitudes. Arabov's former wife must have seen the same thing – she suddenly began to cry from her eternal grief and turned away, feeling ashamed before these strangers. She knew instinctively that there can be no help from others and that it's best to hide away on one's own.

Upset by all this, Grunyakhin went out onto the street with Katya and said to her, "You've heard of the golden rule of mechanics. Some people have thought they can use this rule to cheat the whole of nature, the whole of life. Kostya Arabov wanted to obtain with you, or from you – how can I put it? – some kind of free gold. And he did find a little."

"A little – yes," Katya agreed.

"But how much? Not more than a gram. And to achieve equilibrium it was necessary to weigh down the other end of the lever with a whole ton of the graveyard earth that now lies on top of his son and crushes him."

Katya Bessonet frowned in bewilderment.

"Don't ever try to live by the golden rule," Grunyakhin went on. "It's an ignorant way to live, and it'll make you unhappy. I'm an engineer, I can tell you: nature's something altogether more serious. You can't play games with nature. Well, goodbye now – here's your bus."

"Wait," said Katya Bessonet.

"I haven't got time," said Grunyakhin. "I'm not interested, I don't like it when people get drunk on themselves and then turn to me because they don't know what to do with themselves any more. One should live more correctly."

Katya laughed unexpectedly. "All right, all right," she said.

"The way you come out with all these demands, anyone would think it was me who made me the way I am. I'm not this way on purpose – far from it. But it won't happen again, I'm sorry . . ."

Grunyakhin went back to the room of Arabov's wife. She met him with her former indifference, but he, as he crossed the threshold, suggested she marry him: he had nothing else to offer. The woman went pale, as if struck by a sudden illness, and said nothing. Grunyakhin stayed there, sitting in the room till it was late at night and the traffic outside came to a stop. Then he fell asleep without meaning to, and Arabov's wife arranged some bedding for him on the short sofa and told him to lie down properly.

In the morning Grunyakhin went to work as usual, but in the evening he came back. Matryona Filippovna Cheburkova (she had stopped using her husband's surname after being betrayed by him) neither greeted this new man nor drove him away. He gave her some money, putting it on the table; mechanically, she made him some tea and warmed up the left-overs from her own supper. A few days later the janitor came round in the evening and told Matryona Filippovna to get her new tenant registered: really, of course, it was up to her – she could marry him or she could send him packing – but living like this was impermissible. The janitor was a dispossessed *kulak*, and so he observed the law with extreme punctiliousness: he had himself experienced and survived the power of the State.

"You watch out, citizen Cheburkova, or you'll get yourself fined. The State doesn't like to lose out!"

"All right then. In the past I wouldn't have got fined – but now that I'm weak and without a husband . . ."

"Well, get him registered!" The janitor pointed at Grunyakhin. "Don't lose what you're entitled to as a married wife. If you lose your living space, you'll end up like Little Dumpling in the film[36] – except you're too thin!"

"You can register him tomorrow – there's plenty of time," said Cheburkova. "Nowadays women need to think things over."

"So I see!" said the janitor, and left. From the other side of the door he added, "In the past women didn't do any thinking at all, but they lived free of stupidity, the same as if they were clever."

Two days later Grunyakhin got himself registered as a temporary tenant, but Cheburkova told him to register for a permanent life. Who's going to believe that a man and a woman are living separately in a single room with a kitchen?" she said irritably. "And I'm not just a girl off the street – I'm a woman. Tomorrow you're going to the registry office with me – I swear by my life! Or else you can go back where you came from!"

Everything was done correctly and quickly, and Grunyakhin's life settled down in another person's room. He worked, Matryona Filippovna did the housework, expressed various discontents, and occasionally spoke of her son – most likely just so as to feel, after her tears, the relief which is equivalent to heart-felt joy; she was not able to experience any other happiness, or had never had the chance to. Without her realizing it, her son's death gradually became the source of a quiet happiness in her life – a happiness that came after brief tears, in slow, detailed recollections. And she would invite Grunyakhin to share in her impoverished feelings, which nevertheless included not only the comforting warmth that came from this dark intoxication with her own sorrow, but also all the endurance of her soul. At times like this she became kinder and meeker than her character demanded. Grunyakhin even liked it when Matryona Filippovna suddenly began to cry about her dead child – some little favour, some kind of tenderness from his wife would then come his way.

As a rule, Cheburkova did not allow her husband to go anywhere except to work, and she would keep an eye on the clock: would he be back home on time? She did not believe in official meetings, and she would begin weeping and cursing, saying that her second husband was a scoundrel too and that he was betraying her. If her husband still came in late, Matryona Filippovna would open the door and set about him, using an old felt boot, a coat rail together with its clothes, a flue from what had once been a samovar, a shoe off her own foot, or any immediate thing she could lay her hands on – anything to exhaust her own irritation and unhappiness. During such moments Grunyakhin would look at Matryona Filippovna with surprise, while she cried pathetically – because one grief had simply turned into another, and had not disappeared completely. Grunyakhin, who had seen much of life, was not especially upset at being treated like this.

Matryona Filippovna's second son would watch these quarrels between his mother and his new father without emotion, since his mother always had the advantage. But once, when Grunyakhin seized his wife's hands because she had started tearing at his throat with her finger nails, the boy gave him this warning: "Comrade Grunyakhin, don't you hit my Mum! Or I'll skewer you through the guts with an awl, you son of a bitch! You're not in your own home now – you'd better learn your place!"

Grunyakhin immediately came to his senses; it was only inadvertently, and because of severe pain, that he had forgotten himself. It was in the hot sweat of despair, in exhaustion, with the zeal of her whole heart that Matryona Filippovna got so upset with him – she was defending her husband from vice and ensuring his fidelity to his family. Grunyakhin listened, endured and learned.

At night, beside his wife, he thought that everything was as it should be; otherwise his light and greedy heart would quickly have exhausted itself and perished in fruitless attachment to a variety of women and friends, in a dangerous readiness to throw itself into the thick of all the luxury that ever happens on earth.

In the morning the son – whose name was Semyon, just as Grunyakhin's had once been – said to Ivan Stepanovich, "Why do you sleep with my mother? Do you think I enjoy watching you? Yes or no?"

Grunyakhin was abashed by the question. His wife was not there; she had gone to the market for food. It was the beginning of a day off work, when people live by domestic feelings and shared thoughts and take their children to the cinema. Grunyakhin and Semyon went to the cinema too, to watch a Soviet comedy. Semyon was content enough, although he criticized the film; to him the problems in it seemed petty – he had lived through worse himself. At home Matryona Filippovna was sitting and crying in front of a picture of her past husband; then she saw Grunyakhin, felt ashamed, and stopped. Grunyakhin had no need of any greater love; he saw Matryona Filippovna's awkwardness as the mark of a meek trust, a supreme tenderness towards him. He took no account of his sufferings at the hands of this woman: people had not yet attained the courage of continual happiness – they were only learning.

At night, after his wife and son had gone to sleep, Grunyakhin would bend over Matryona Filippovna's face and observe how entirely helpless she was, how pathetically her face had tensed in miserable exhaustion, while her eyes were closed as if they were kind eyes, as if some ancient angel were resting in her while she lay unconscious. If all of humanity were lying still and sleeping, it would be impossible to judge its real character from its face and one could be deceived.

NOTES

PREFACE AND INTRODUCTION

1 Aleksandr Pushkin, *Eugene Onegin*, tr. V. Nabokov, Princeton, 1990, p. 141.

2 Several interesting articles have appeared in Russia about the influence of Russian philosophers and, in particular, of Solovyov and Fyodorov, on *Happy Moscow*. These include Natasha Drubek-Meyer, "Rossiya – 'pustota v kishkakh' mira", *Novoe literaturnoe obozrenie*, 1994, no.9, pp.251–268; Svetlana Semenova, "Filosofskie motivy romana *Schastlivaya Moskva*", and Evgeny Yablokov, "Schast'e i neschast'e Moskvy ('Moskovskie' syuzhety u A. Platonova i B. Pil'nyaka)", in N. V. Kornienko, ed, "Strana Filosofov": *Andreya Platonova: problemy tvorchestva*, vyp.2, (Moscow: Nasledie, 1995), pp.54–90 and 221–239.

3 Aleksandr Blok, "Poeziya zagovorov i zaklinaniy", *Sobranie sochineniy v vos'mi tomakh* (Moscow: Khudozhestvennaya literatura, 1960–63), vol.1, pp.36–65. For an excellent discussion of the incantatory function in Russian modernism, see also, Gregory Freidin, *A Coat of Many Colors: Osip Mandelstam and his Mythologies of Self-Presentation* (Berkeley: University of California Press, 1987).

4 The ultimate verbalist manifesto of the pre-Revolutionary decade is probably Andrey Bely's "The Magic of Words". *Simvolizm kak miroponimanie* (Moscow: Respublika, 1994), pp.131–142.

5 See Trotsky's hostile comments in his *Literatura i revolyutsiya* (Moscow: Politicheskaya literatura, 1991 [1923]), pp.49–54, 107–8.

6 In an early article, Platonov expressed his appreciation of journalism's militant ideological role. "Gazeta i ee znachenie", *Krasnaya derevnya*, no.163, 23 September 1920, p.2.

7 I. V. Stalin, *Sochineniya* (Moscow: Gosudarstvennoe izdatel'stvo, 1949), vol.12, p.191.

8 In Stalin's attack on Bukharin at the Party plenum in 1928, from which the quotation is taken, the latter's chief fault was his failure to grasp the Party's slogans; a major error of Bukharin and his followers was that they *talked* about the wrong things. *Sochineniya*, vol.12, pp.10–11.

9 E. D. Shubina, "Sozertsatel' i deiatel'", in N. V. Kornienko and E. D. Shubina (eds.), *Andrey Platonov: Vospominaniya sovremennikov: Materialy k biografii* (Moscow: Sovremenniy pisatel', 1994), pp.139–40.

10 The history of Platonov's relationship with Gorky is discussed by Lev Anninsky in his article "Otkrovenie i sokrovenie (Gor'ky i Platonov)", *Literaturnoe obozrenie*, 1989, no.9, pp.3–21.

11 N. V. Kornienko, ". . . Na krayu sobstvennogo bezmolviya", *Novy mir*, 1991, no.9, pp.58–62.

12 Mikhail Geller and Aleksandr Nekrich, *Utopiya u vlasti* (London: Overseas Publications, 1982), vol.1, p.296.

13 Randi Barnes Cox, "Toiling Masses and Cultured Shoppers: Images of Consumption and Identity in Soviet Commercial Advertising, 1922–1941", forthcoming in Christina Kiaer and Eric Naiman (eds.), *Everyday Revolution: Formations of Identity in Soviet Russia*.

14 Stalin, *Sochineniya*, vol.14, p.63. (Volumes 14–16 of Stalin's collected works were published by the Hoover Institute at Stanford in 1967.)

15 Stalin, *Sochineniya*, vol.14, p.106.

16 Vadim Volkov, "The Concept of Kul'turnost': Notes on the Stalinist Civilizing Process", in Kiaer and Naiman, *Everyday Revolution*; Sheila Fitzpatrick, "Becoming Cultured: Socialist Realism and the Representation of Privilege and Taste", in her *The Cultural Front: Power and Culture in Revolutionary Russia* (Ithaca: Cornell University Press, 1992) pp.216–237.

17　Stalin, *Sochineniya*, vol.14, p.81.

18　See the description of the conditions of daily life provided by Sheila Fitzpatrick in her *Everyday Stalinism: Ordinary Life in Extraordinary Times: Soviet Russia in the 1930s* (New York: Oxford University Press, 1999), pp.40–66.

19　Wolfgang Leonhard, *Child of the Revolution*, trans. C. M. Woodhouse (Chicago: Henry Regnery, 1958), pp.21–22.

20　The story is translated in *The Portable Platonov*, tr. R. & E. Chandler et al. (Moscow: Glas, 1999).

21　Andrey Platonov, "O pervoy sotsialisticheskoy tragediey", *Russkaya literatura*, 1993, no.2, p.204.

22　Moscow's collective role is discussed by Evgeny Yablokov in "Schast'e i neschast'e Moskvy", pp.223–4.

23　This point is particularly stressed by Svetlana Semyonova, "Filosofskie motivy", pp. 66–67, 83.

24　Platonov was struck by many of Weininger's themes and arguments, but he found the conclusions drawn by him to be tragic and abhorrent. Yury Nagibin recalls that Platonov spoke about Weininger "so tenderly and sympathetically, that it was as if the young, misguided Weininger were crying in the next room", "Eshcho o Platonove", in Kornienko and Shubina (eds.) *Andrey Platonov: Vospominaniya sovremennikov*, p.75.

25　This point is also made by Evgeny Yablokov, "Schast'e i neschast'e Moskvy", p.226.

26　Thomas Seifrid draws fascinating parallels between the ideological significance of filth in the works of Platonov and Georges Bataille. "Smradnye radosti marksizma: zametki o Platonove i Batae", *Novoe literaturnoe obozrenie*, 1998, no.32, pp.48–59. See also his treatment of the chthonic elements in Platonov's writing in his monograph, *Andrey Platonov: Uncertainties of Spirit* (Cambridge University Press, 1992). In a recent article, Keith Livers sheds interesting light on the relationship of filth to redemption in *Happy Moscow* and in other works by Platonov from the late 1930s. "Scatology and Eschatology: The Recovery of the Flesh in Andrei Platonov's *Happy Moscow*", *Slavic Review*, vol.59, no.1 (2000), pp.154–182.

27 In keeping with this dynamic, it is quite natural that when Sartorius attempts to chat up a woman employed in the construction of the Moscow Metro, this worker with an ideologically alluring occupation is described as "dirty and beautiful".

28 Vladimir Solovyov, "Smysl lyubvi", in his *Sochineniya v dvukh tomakh* (Moscow: Mysl', 1988), vol.2, p.540.

29 Sambikin's discovery is consistent with a 1921 article by Platonov about a stubborn, "indecently" pure young communist rebuked by his co-workers because he dwells "in the water closet" of the soul rather than in its "drawing rooms and halls" as do more conventional folk. Andrey Platonov, "Dusha cheloveka – neprilichnoe zhivotnoe", in his *Vozvrashchenie* (Moscow: Molodaya gvardiya, 1989), p.36.

30 In 1934 Platonov published a version of the second chapter as a short story. The opening sentence there read "In Moscow, on the seventh floor, lived a 30-year-old man, Viktor Vasilievich Bozhko." Thomas Seifrid has singled out that sentence as representative of Platonov's style: "In this locution, whose semantic effects precipitate out of an 'illiterate' failure to mention the building in which the hero lives, it is as though Moscow were conceived of as a single building (an echo, perhaps of the Proletarian Home in [*The Foundation Pit*]), and the hero were not an individual Bozhko but 'humankind' itself." *Andrey Platonov: Uncertainties of Spirit*, p.200. Among the redundant words making frequent appearances in Happy Moscow, the most prominent are "life" (for example "in the youth of his life" instead of "in his youth" and "time" ("grieving so badly for the time of her past" instead of "grieving so badly for her past").

31 Yury Nagibin, "Samiy strashniy roman Andreya Platonova",

Literaturnaya gazeta, 2 May 1992, p.4.

32 Stalin, *Sochineniya*, vol.14, pp.87–8.

33 Kornienko, ". . . Na krayu sobstvennogo bezmolviya", p.59.

34 Keith Livers also draws attention to the potential autobiographical significance of this poster. "Scatology and Eschatology", p.179.

HAPPY MOSCOW

1 Moscow's last name is formed from "*chestny*", which means "honest". In an early draft, her name was to have been "Yavnaya" – "clear". N. V. Kornienko, ". . . Na krayu sobstvennogo bezmolviya", *Novy mir*, 1991:9, p.60.

2 Aleksey Vasilevich Kol'tsov (1809–43), a poet born in Platonov's native town of Voronezh, was famous for his songs, which drew heavily on folk and popular elements.

3 Bozhko's name is formed from "Bozhok", a diminutive form of the word for "god" (*bog*), which also means a small idol or a person worthy of adoration.

4 In the 1920s there was much Soviet interest in Esperanto as an international workers' language. Proponents of Esperanto claimed that the language was an ideal way of informing the working class in other countries about the achievements of workers in the USSR. Accordingly, in 1926, with the blessing of *Izvestiya* and the Komsomol, massive Esperanto letter-writing campaigns were begun in many Soviet cities; replies from foreign workers were published in the Soviet press. Correspondence between Soviet and foreign workers came under much tighter control in the early 1930s; letter writing was strictly organized to minimize negative comments by Soviet citizens about their standard of living, and Soviet Esperantists were issued model answers to difficult questions they might receive from their foreign correspondents. The Union of Soviet Esperantists counted over 13,000 members by 1935, but the movement was virtually non-existent a

few years later. Although there was never any formal campaign against Esperanto, the movement was decimated during the Purges, when epistolary contact with foreigners was used as a criterion for arrest. (Bozhko would certainly have been arrested in 1937.) The history of Esperanto in the Soviet Union is told by Ulrich Lins in *Die Gefaehrliche Sprache: Die Verfolgung der Esperantisten unter Hitler und Stalin*. (Gerlingen: Bleicher, 1988).

5 i.e. an exemplary worker. Stakhanov was a coal miner whose improbably huge output of coal was held up as a model for workers.

6 Every institute, factory, etc, would produce its own "wall news-paper" – effectively a newsletter, full of the appropriate propaganda, that would be pasted up on the wall at regular intervals.

7 The Society for the Promotion of Defence, Aviation and Chemistry (*Obshchestvo sodeistviya oborone i aviatsionno-khimich-eskomu stroitel'stvu*). A "voluntary" civil defence organization which promoted patriotism, marksmanship and aviation skills among the general populace. Founded in 1927, it was described by Stalin as vital to "keeping the entire population in a state of mobilized readiness against the danger of military attack, so that no 'accident' and no tricks of our external enemies can catch us unawares." In furtherance of this mission, the Society sponsored clubs and organized contests throughout the USSR. By 1929, there were around 12 million members. *Bol'shaya sovetskaya entsiklopediya*, (Moscow: Sovetskaya entsiklopediya, 1926–47), 1st ed., vol.55, pp.468–69.

8 The profession of parachutist was an ideologically glamorous one in the 1930s; parachute-jumping was also widely practised by amateurs, as a sport and as a form of civil defence training. The Society for the Promotion of Defence, Aviation and Chemistry established the order of "Master of Parachute Sport in the USSR", and national competitions began in 1935. One of the most famous parachutists was Lyubov' Berlin, the first woman, *Pravda* claimed,

to parachute from a glider. She and her close friend, Tamara Ivanova, were killed on 26 March 1936 in the course of a jump with special late-opening parachutes. Their pictures were published in *Pravda* and their bodies lay in state in the Moscow Press House; the two were hailed by *Pravda* as "young, energetic, fearless daughters of the Lenin Komsomol" (28 March 1936, p.4). Given the date of Platonov's first sketches for *Happy Moscow*, the urban connection between his heroine's name and that of comrade Berlin is probably coincidental.

9 i.e. the best, most exemplary members of the labour force, by analogy with *shock troops*.

10 The Union of Communist Youth.

11 The Russian word "*vnevoiskovik*" literally means someone who is "outside the army." Although it did not have such a connotation in everyday life, in the context of this novel it ought, perhaps, to be read as referring to a person who is "outside of the struggle", not fighting to further the Bolshevik cause.

12 Usually referred to by its acronym, MOPR, the International Organization of Aid for the Fighters of the Revolution (*Mezhdu-narodnaya organizatsiya pomoshchi bortsam revoliutsii*). Founded by the Comintern in 1922, this organization collected funds to publicize the plight of political prisoners in capitalist countries and to provide material assistance to the families of imprisoned or murdered revolutionaries. In 1932 MOPR counted 9.7 million Soviet citizens among its members. *Bol'shaya sovetskaya entsiklopediya*, (Moscow: Sovetskaya entsiklopediya, 1969–81), 3rd ed., vol.15, p.593.

13 i.e. he received the minimum State pension.

14 Nikolay Mikhailovich Yazykov (1803–47). A contemporary of Pushkin. The quoted lines are taken from his 1829 poem, *Plovets* (The Sailor), which promises sailors that if they remain "strong in soul" they will survive the coming storm. Platonov has added a syllable to the third line, which undercuts the rhythm (and

perhaps, the promise) of this hopeful stanza.

15 Soviet science was profoundly interested in the notion of "rejuvenation". In the 1920s the Soviet popular press paid a great deal of attention to the medical procedures developed by Eugen Steinach in Austria and Sergei Voronoff in France. Both doctors argued that the aging human organism could be revived by simple operations involving the sex glands: Steinach tied off the vas deferens to transform the testes into an organ of heightened internal secretion for the revitalization of the entire organism. Voronoff founded a clinic in Menton where he grafted material from the sex glands of primates into hundreds of human patients. The centre of Soviet research on rejuvenation was Nikolay Kol'tsov's Institute of Experimental Biology. In the 1930s, attention shifted to other revitalizing processes. Aleksey Zamkov, a disciple of Kol'tsov, developed "gravidan", a filtration of the urine of pregnant women, which so impressed Gorky that he persuaded the Politburo to establish a Scientific Research Institute devoted entirely to the treatment of a wide range of medical conditions with gravidan. Gravidan was used to treat a variety of conditions, ranging from glaucoma to cancer. Experimental treatments of this kind – in effect a medical version of Social Realism – received substantial coverage in the leading papers and journals of the day. Clint Walker has pointed out (in "Unmasking the Myths and Metaphors of the Stalinist Utopia", *Essays in Poetics*, Keele, 2001, note 44) that an article was published in January 1935, in the "Science and Technology" column of *Izvestiya*, entitled "Necrobiotic Rays" and detailing the discovery of "an emanation released by living organisms at the moment of death and called necrobiotic rays".

16 In the early 1930s, unable to support his family by writing, Platonov worked as a senior engineer in the Russian Federation's "Republican Trust for the Production and Repair of Scales and

Measures" (*Rosmetroves*), Kornienko, ". . . Na krayu sobstvennogo bezmolviya", p.60.

17 Sentence unfinished in manuscript.

18 A famous clock tower in the Kremlin. During the thirties, before closing down for the night, the State radio would broadcast its bells chiming midnight and then playing the Internationale.

19 Early Soviet anti-religious propaganda attempted to reduce the traditional notion of the soul to physiological processes. In the 1920s, endocrinologists claimed that the soul was nothing more than glandular function. The location of the soul in the intestinal tract is probably Platonov's own "discovery".

20 A distorted echo of the claim made in *The Brothers Karamazov* that reformers who seek to feed the poor will never accomplish anything if they do not believe in God. One should also note the paradoxical link, drawn by Dostoevsky in the same novel, between purity of the soul and the stench of putrefaction.

21 The construction of the Moscow Metro began in 1932 and was portrayed as a significant part of Stalin's plans for the physical transformation of the entire city. A massive campaign to bring more workers to the construction sites began in 1933. The first line – 11.6 kilometres of track and 13 stations – was completed within the astonishingly short period of three years. The stations were described by the *Bol'shaya Sovetskaia Entsiklopediya* as "joyful palaces" that reflected the spirit of the socialist epoch (1st ed. vol.39, p. 213). Clint Walker points out (op.cit.) that an article was published in *Izvestiya* on 8 March 1935 (International Women's Day) relating how a group of female Komosol members volunteered for work in the shafts and tunnels of the Metro. "At first they were turned away at the gates with the phrase 'Women aren't allowed!'. The zealous young women refused to take no for an answer, however: 'We've already been on the surface, comrades. I've already jumped three times with a parachute, how can I go higher than

that? Now let me go below, under the ground'." The women, of course, are taken on, and one of them is praised for being able to keep her hair perfectly clean even though she is working deep underground.

22 A reference to Stalin's February 1931 speech "About Economic Tasks", where he called for maximal intervention in economic production: "It is time to finish with that rotten policy of nonintervention in production. It is time to master a new policy that corresponds to the situation of today: intervene in everything." Stalin, Collected Works . . . 13:410, quoted in Kornienko, ". . . Na krayu sobstvennogo bezmolviya", p.64. Platonov is also alluding to the doctrines of Socialist Realism: the task assigned to writers was the engineering of human souls.

23 A famous pilot in the Soviet Air Force, the holder of world records for high-altitude flight. Killed in a flying accident in 1934.

24 A Fyodorovan revision of Jesus's words in Matthew 8:22: "Let the dead bury their dead."

25 i.e. representatives of the Party, the trade union, and management.

26 Somewhat improbably, 40 pounds!

27 The phrase *elections to a constituent assembly* was omitted in Platonov's final draft. We have chosen to reinstate it, as its omission may have been an act of self-censorship. It would have been suicidally audacious to allude in this way to the fate of the Constituent Assembly elected in late 1917. The Bolsheviks gained less than a quarter of the votes to this first democratically elected Russian parliament. Rather than remain a minority in government, they broke up the first session, using the Red Guards to disband the delegates.

28 Here we have translated the original version of a sentence which Platonov went on to revise. His final version could be translated as: *And if anyone did live that way, all they could do was turn goggle-eyed and stupefied from imbecility.* The original version seems to work

better, at least in English.

29 Several railway termini are located on this square.

30 Sartorius's failure to recognize Komyagin's name and address is surprising. It could be explained as stemming from a wish on Sartorius's part not to acknowledge that he is in the presence of Moscow Chestnova's lover. Or it may simply be a slip on Platonov's part.

31 Anatoly Lunacharsky (1875–1933) was appointed Commissar for Education and the Arts in 1917. Clint Walker (op.cit.) discusses Platonov's long-running polemic with Lunacharsky, one of the first and most vehement advocates of "a practical, technical culture", "a great organizing force" that would transform not only the external environment but also the souls of the Soviet people.

32 The Donets Basin, the centre of the Soviet Union's coal, iron and steel production.

33 Like so many apparently strange or surreal passages in Platonov, this passage is in fact extremely realistic. Sheila Fitzpatrick (*Everyday Stalinism*, New York, O.U.P., 1999, p.132–7), brings home how frequently Soviet citizens with a dubious past – e.g. former priests and *kulaks*, and their families – attempted to take on new identities in precisely this way, though of course for different reasons. Sartorius's name is almost certainly derived from that of the title character of Thomas Carlyle's philosophical novel, *Sartor Resartus* [The Tailor Retailored]. Like Carlyle's hero, Sartorius renounces his own self, along with all individualistic striving towards an increase in one's personal happiness. See Clint Walker (op.cit., note 46).

34 A suburb of Moscow.

35 Platonov mentions a hydraulic pump called "Bessonet-Favor" in his article "Goryachaya Arktika" (Andrey Platonov, "Chutyo pravdy" (Moscow, Sovetskaya Rossiya, 1990). In *Happy Moscow* this name perhaps functions as a kind of pun. As Natalya Kornienko points

out (Andrey Platonov, *Zapisnye knizhki*, p.380, note 82), the name recalls the achievements of world technology. At the same time, it is erotically charged. Bessonet is reminiscent of the French *besogne*, meaning "need" or even "sexual intercourse"; Favor sounds like *faveur*, meaning "favour" or "gift", often in an amorous context.

36 A reference to *Pyshka*, Mikhail Romm's 1934 cinematic version of Maupassant's "Boule de suif". "Boule de suif" – in Russian she was given the somewhat more attractive name of *Pyshka* or *Little Dumpling* – is the name of an amply endowed, kind-hearted and patriotically minded French prostitute whose sacrifices for the common good are insufficiently appreciated by her bourgeois travelling companions.